Desert Guns

Desert Guns

STEVE FRAZEE

Thorndike Press • **Chivers Press**
Thorndike, Maine USA **Bath, England**

This Large Print edition is published by Thorndike Press, USA and by Chivers Press, England.

Published in 1998 in the U.S. by arrangement with Golden West Literary Agency.

Published in 1998 in the U.K. by arrangement with Golden West Literary Agency.

U.S. Hardcover 0-7862-1350-7 (Western Series Edition)
U.K. Hardcover 0-7540-3228-0 (Chivers Large Print)
U.K. Softcover 0-7540-3229-9 (Camden Large Print)

Copyright © 1957 by Steve Frazee
Copyright © 1961 by Steve Frazee in the British Commonwealth
Copyright © renewed 1985 by Steve Frazee

All rights reserved.

Thorndike Large Print® Western Series.

The text of this edition is unabridged.
Other aspects of the book may vary from the original edition.

Set in 16 pt. Plantin by Al Chase.

Printed in the United States on permanent paper.

British Library Cataloguing in Publication Data available

Library of Congress Cataloging in Publication Data
Frazee, Steve, 1909–
    Desert guns / by Steve Frazee.
        p. cm.
    ISBN 0-7862-1350-7 (lg. print : hc : alk. paper)
    I. Large type books. I. Title.
[PS3556.R358D47   1998]
    813'.54—dc21   97-43871

Desert Guns

CHAPTER ONE

They had seldom run from Indians the way they were running now from something Shaun Weymouth had seen out in the great San Luis Valley where the sage flowed into distance against the far La Garita Mountains. Jim Rainbolt had been with Shaun long enough to move swiftly when Shaun moved, to run first and ask questions later.

The year was 1853. They were on the boundary between Kansas and New Mexico Territories, but of such matters they knew little and cared less.

Their Indian ponies were tired. The grass had just been coming on when they left the snug pocket in the hills where they had wintered on a nameless branch of the River of Lost Souls. Not much at best, the scrubby calico packhorse traded from one of Mano's bucks was proof that Ute ponies were not meant to carry dead weight at a fast clip over a great distance.

The calico was faltering for a good reason. It had packed more than two hundred and fifty pounds of gold from the San Juan in five days of hard riding.

Shaun left the piñons suddenly and slid

his pony down a bank into a broad, sandy gulch. He waited while Rainbolt tried to tow the packhorse over the edge. The calico braced against the descent and tried to go along the bank instead. Sand sprayed from the hoofs of Shaun's pony as he wheeled back to help.

He and Rainbolt dragged the packhorse into the gulch, and then Shaun rode behind it.

"What is it, Utes?" Rainbolt asked.

"Worse," Shaun grunted. "I think it's white men."

Rainbolt asked no more as he hauled the calico on. He was a raw-boned, angular man with a heavy facial structure that needed more flesh upon it if anyone was to call him handsome. A shock of auburn hair was escaping at the edges of his greasy, weather-rent hat. His gray eyes were dust-rimmed and bloodshot from the alkali flats of the valley. The night before at the lonely ranch where they had stopped with a man named Hudson and his daughter, Rainbolt had shaved for the first time in months; and now the lack of whiskers emphasized the harsh lines of his face.

He was twenty-six years old, as close as he could remember. He had been about eighteen when he looked for the last time at a sunset from his father's farm near Vincennes, and said, "I'm going out there tomorrow, Pa. I'm old enough and I've waited long enough."

And the next day he had left, green and strong and ready to show all Indians how the boar ate the cabbage.

Beside Shaun Weymouth, Rainbolt was still a young, green boy; and this in spite of the fact that he had learned much of the frontier before he ever met Shaun, and a great deal more during the three years he and Shaun had ranged together.

Shaun, too, had shaved the night before at the Hudson place and he had knifed off some of his mane of coal-black hair. In spite of the recent loss of his beard, his skin was dark, and it lay with youthful tightness against his square-hewn features. He was past fifty, but he was old only in the aggressive wiseness of his wrinkled eyes and in the hard set of his mouth. His buckskins were dark down the front from blood and grease and usage. He wore moccasins and he used a nose hitch on his pony instead of a bridle.

For thirty of his fifty some years Shaun had been a trespasser in Indian country; he had trespassed so long that he had nearly been absorbed.

The urgency in him now was puzzling.

From the Little Missouri to Taos he and Rainbolt had never run in desperation before, but only as a matter of necessity. You could almost say that Shaun was afraid.

Rainbolt said, "You think they're from the camp where we saw that fellow on the pass coming out of the San Juan?"

"Sure of it." Shaun lashed the packhorse. It lurched ahead and a wind from the southwest lifted its mane.

For miles the dunes had been in sight — brown, enormous hills in an angle of the Blood of Christ Mountains.

Riding down the distance toward them, Rainbolt had thought the dunes would never come closer. They had been like a mirage: constant in the vision, but receding, mocking approach, holding space between them and their viewer. But now the distance had been conquered. Hurried by Shaun's urging, Rainbolt pushed his pony rapidly through the ever-deepening flow of sand from the skirts of the dunes, and through the trees that lined the gulch he kept getting imperfect glimpses of the pale-brown hills.

Rainbolt rode free of the gulch and had his first close and unobstructed view of the upswooped ridges before him, tawny in the full strike of the sun, shifting to delicate shades of brown in the shadows. The south shoulder of the dunes, on Rainbolt's right, was close to the mountains where the passes lay. But on the left from this blunt angle the sand blocked for miles all view of the mountains to the north.

Wind-sculptured into curving smoothness, the ridges of sand rose seven hundred feet toward the sky. Rainbolt saw the wind racing on the delicate spines, laying the sand before it like the manes of wild-running horses.

No tree or rock or permanency of any kind broke the flowing architecture. There was only sand that for a million years had been gathered here by wind currents sweeping across the great San Luis Valley.

Rainbolt paid brief respects to the beauty of the dunes. He looked behind him. Shaun was lashing the calico again. Pastern deep, the little pony came plopping through the sand.

Rainbolt looked up the passes, off to the right — Mosca, Medano and Music. He had never crossed any of them but Shaun knew the way.

From the day they had first met on the Sweetwater, Shaun had been the leader, as befitted his age and experience; and Rainbolt had never had cause to question his judgment. They had come together in a trapper's camp where a Spanish trader was selling powder and lead and whisky. During a high afternoon of celebration Shaun had beaten every trapper at Indian wrestling.

Then Rainbolt took him on in a match and rolled him up like a sleeping cub bear. The trappers howled with glee. From Indian wrestling Shaun and Rainbolt, excited and half angry, went on into a serious fight. They were trying to kill each other when they rolled over a steep bank and fell into the river, and even then they kept on fighting until they were drowning.

When they staggered ashore, they were too weak to fight any more. They looked at each other and began to laugh. Two days later they left the camp in partnership.

Since then Rainbolt had never seen such a brittle edge on Shaun as there was now. He turned again to look at Shaun, and the older man motioned him to greater speed with a Sioux hand signal.

For a while Rainbolt thought they were going around the shoulder of the dunes and up toward one of the passes. It was the only way they could go.

Shaun said, "Hold up." He stepped off his pony and led it toward the lightning-blasted trunk of a cottonwood. He pointed straight toward the dunes where the first ridge of sand lifted ten feet high. On beyond that, curving upward in a graceful sweep, was a long spine.

No horses would ever cross those dunes, and Rainbolt knew it. Again Shaun gave him a sign, straight ahead toward the first low ridge. Rainbolt gave the tow rope a jerk and obeyed. He kept looking toward the valley. He saw the rabbit brush, the sage, a great dust cloud whirling across an alkali flat, and the blueness of faraway mountains marking the beginning of the San Juan.

For a while the dust cloud held his interest narrowly, but it was nothing. The wind was blowing steadily. From here to the La Garitas there could be a hundred dust clouds like that.

He struck the low ridge and then he was in trouble. The pony tried to lunge through and couldn't make it. Rainbolt left it standing knee deep in sand that ran like water. He went back and concentrated on the packhorse. Terrified by the shifting softness, the calico held back, rolling its eyes and bracing against the tow rope.

With Ute cruelty Rainbolt made it move. He forced it over the ridge, plunging down into a cove swept clean of sand by the wind. The bottom was bare rock, with a trace of vegetation in the hard soil. Rising steeply on three sides were sand slopes. No horse could go any farther than this.

Rainbolt went back for the other pony. Shaun was leading his horse at an even pace. Once more Rainbolt looked out into the valley and saw no definite signs of danger. But when they were both in the hollow, with Shaun lying near the top of the western rim of the hollow, Shaun said, "They're coming. White men."

Rainbolt scrambled up and lay down beside him. After several minutes Rainbolt said he could not see riders.

"I don't neither — right now," Shaun grunted. "Take the gold off the calico."

Rainbolt lifted one side of the panniers and let the whole weight fall. It struck with a soft thump. Dust and nuggets were bagged inside the panniers in twenty wheels of buckskin.

Staring into the wind, his vision troubled a little by the heat waves in the valley, Shaun was thinking about the gold in the panniers. A big fortune, more than a man rightly knew what to do with. Furs were different. You never got so many of them or such a solid weight of them that you felt all bogged down. Gold was a hell of a thing to have and worse not to have.

Again Shaun saw the thin smoke of the dust of riding men. They weren't making a race of it but they were coming along steady and sure, and all crowded up in a bunch the way white men rode. If there wasn't so much wind, Rainbolt would have seen too. Rainbolt was all right.

He was young, of course, and things like gold meant a heap to you when you were young. Shaun guessed the gold meant quite a lot to him, too. A man got old. His bones ached sometimes and he never let on. Indian women didn't look as good as they once did. You got tired and it was time to light somewhere and spin big lies to wide-eyed youngsters.

Shaun guessed he would have enjoyed it well enough, settling down on a little farm somewhere in Missouri, say, with maybe a couple of good slaves that he wouldn't work too hard. It might have been fairly pleasant, at that.

But when your string ran out, you settled right where things ended. You went under and that was it. Somewhere between this pile of sand and the Huerfano, Shaun Weymouth was going under.

It was a feeling. You didn't go against strong feelings and last thirty years in Indian country, not against the Sarsi and the Bloods and a few other hair-lifters Shaun had seen in his time. A feeling was everything. It woke you in the night and you knew a long-haired Crow was after your horses. You looked at a hill and you had a feeling about which side wasn't going to be safe to ride around.

Shaun watched the valley. He saw the dust again, quick rising, swept away low against the ground before it had a chance to stand in the air like a smoke signal. Sure, they were on the trail, headed dead-on toward the Hudson ranch.

Rainbolt came over and lay down beside Shaun.

"Dust running close to the ground," Shaun said. "Catch the line of it two, three times and then you know where it's going to show again." There was a heap of dust out in the valley now, as the wind primed itself to come booming in against the mountains.

"Suppose they ain't after us?" Rainbolt asked.

"Then the rest is doing the horses good. Tell you now that calico couldn't beat 'em over the hill with the pack he's got if we'd started to run for it two hours ago."

"Where do we fight 'em?"

"Want to be right first," Shaun said. He knew that Rainbolt still hadn't seen the dust. Knowing where to look for danger was sort of a feeling too. It didn't come on a man all at once; he earned it by getting arrows shafted into him, by crawling away from a camp in the dead of night when he knew they had him beat, by killing without warning or mercy when killing was necessary — it came from many things that Rainbolt still had to learn.

"White men, huh?" Rainbolt asked.

"Sure of it." Shaun rested his eyes by looking at the blue mountains, and then he watched the valley again and picked up the dust right where he knew it would be.

Neither the deep Irish superstition of his boyhood nor the Indian thinking that had crept into his life made him wish to quit before the thing was run clear to the end. He was not like old Thunder, who had declared it was time to die and who had settled down in his lodge on the Rosebud and died within twenty hours.

No, it wasn't like that; they would have a time taking old Shaun Weymouth under. The feeling that had been with him ever since they left the San Juan said that the riders out there would get the job done, sure enough; but Shaun intended to see that it was some doin's.

Too bad it wasn't Indians, or a grizzly, or a deep, swift river you tried to cross one time too many — or any of the things that had a right to kill you. White men putting you under, that was bad.

Right from the first Shaun had known there was something wrong with that gold. It came too easy. It made a man change his whole way of thinking. He began to dream big and the first thing he knew he was thinking about protecting the gold instead of himself.

From the corner of his eye Shaun saw a quick tightening in Rainbolt's attitude. Rainbolt had spotted them now, and a lot sooner at that than Shaun had thought he would.

You could mighty nigh smell the kind that would be riding in that bunch. Green River would be there for sure. It was him that Shaun and Rainbolt had met on the pass coming out of the San Juan. Green River didn't shine no matter how you looked at him. Too bad the Tetons hadn't fixed him for good that time up in the Hole. A man with anything but hog under his hide would have died, what with an arrow through his chest and half his face blowed off with a charge from an English trade musket.

But not Green River. There he'd been, sitting on a log at the break of the pass when Shaun and Rainbolt came up through the dead timber. He made talk out of the good side of his face and his little hog eyes kept sizing up the panniers on the calico like a hungry old squaw looking at a fat white pup.

There was a camp for five, six men in the edge of the timber. Where Green River was, you could bet Frank McCracken wasn't too far off. Too lazy — maybe too smart — to trap, McCracken had been a trader when Shaun first knew him up in Blackfoot country. He was a sight worse than Green River ever could be. McCracken had a dead-cold way of thinking. When he went after something, nothing but brute force could stop him.

Shaun minded the time Buffalo Runs Him and three or four other young Sioux had caught McCracken and two Crows he was trading with for furs. They kept McCracken for the last. They broke the legs and arms of the two Crows and threw them across a fire, pinning them there with heavy poles on the neck and belly. It was normal Sioux fun, if you thought like a Sioux.

Buffalo Runs Him said McCracken watched and listened with a cold face, and when it was his turn he grinned right in the teeth of the young Sioux and told them he was ready. They liked his courage. They let him go free and a half hour later he'd traded them out of the Crow furs without using a drop of whisky.

Sure, McCracken was one of the riders out there. He'd caught the smell of gold in the San Juan, like a hundred others. Only McCracken had come after it without a shovel.

Shaun knew a feeling when he had one. Everything had been bad medicine. The sky hadn't been right the day he and Rainbolt started. Two birds had come low through the trees, fighting in the air. Then they had run smack into Green River when they might have used another pass; but nothing much would have made any difference.

When it was your time to get rubbed out, you knew it. All you could do was to make it as tough as old bull on your enemies. Shaun Weymouth would do that, and he would save the gold for Rainbolt.

The demons of the wind were raising their voices higher. Shaun heard them on the dunes. He knew what the sound was, for he had been here many times before, passing on his way to winter with his friend Dimasio Gondora on the Huerfano. This was the last trip. Shaun felt no regret.

CHAPTER TWO

Rainbolt saw the distant riders clearly enough now. They were going toward the Hudson ranch. If they came away from there in a hurry, the question of their trailing Rainbolt and Shaun would be fairly well settled.

There wasn't a dog's chance of dragging the calico over the mountains with that weight of gold, not in a hurry. Better to make a fight of it, but this was not a good place. They should be up in the timber a ways. Rainbolt still trusted Shaun's judgment but he was not happy about this hole in the sand as a fort-up. No water. No way to run.

Shaun was looking at the distant blue mountains, not at the riders, just staring like there was something out that way that he had not seen before.

Rainbolt slid down the sand and stood by the panniers. What a pile of wealth! First, he'd buy a farm somewhere close to his father's place, and then he'd hire someone to run it. He would get his mother and father whatever they wanted. Why, damn it, he was a wealthy man! It was hard to believe. The most he'd ever had before in all his life was two hundred dollars he'd earned for guiding a wagon train from Leavenworth to Fort Hall four years ago.

Now he was rolling in gold, and when he got back home he'd be something.

Shaun was different. After his first excitement when they found the gold, while not even looking for it, in that little stream down in the San Juan, Shaun had acted funny. He'd kept working away with a fry pan day after day, but he hadn't talked much about what he would do with his share when they got back to the states.

Maybe he'd been so long in the mountains that he didn't realize what gold would buy in the way of happiness.

Rainbolt gave brief consideration to the fact that it had not been the lure of richness that had taken him west seven or eight years back. He had been an ignorant kid who watched the sunsets after a hard day in the field, sensing something big and unknown out there where the light was dying, feeling a mysterious tug. Adventure, maybe it was, calling to him.

Excitement had raced through him when he read stories about Indians and plainsmen in the hay mow after church. All he had known was that he was going west, and making a fortune had not been any great part of it.

That he had the fortune now was more

important than the luck which had given it to him. He kicked the panniers with his foot.

He and Shaun should be getting away, not waiting to make sure about the riders; of course the riders were after this gold.

A weird, whining sort of sound, low and mighty, seemed to come from all around him. He circled the horses. They were standing with their heads lowered toward the rocky floor of the hollow, where only a mouse could have found forage.

Up on the curving ridges that blotted out the mountains the wind was working, swirling, driving across the sand without pattern, whistling, moaning, making strange scratching notes. On the steep sides of the hollow, sand was running like fine brown snow. For one sharp instant Rainbolt thought the great dunes were sliding toward him, spilling down to cover the cove while the sand played its unearthly music.

He bent down to the panniers of gold and stood half crouched as he watched the soft sand moving. It was pouring down from the crests immediately above the hollow but it was not encroaching into the cove because the wind was lifting it as it came down, smoothing it along the sides of the slopes, carrying it toward a bench-like pocket higher up.

Rainbolt looked over the low ridge toward the gulch. Out there on the skirts of the dunes the sand that he and Shaun had crossed was rippled. All tracks were gone.

Rainbolt plunged his hand into the ridge and raked at the sand. He saw it slide silkily back into the hole he had made and the wind poured across the depression and smoothed the last of the mark away.

"Keep down," Shaun said.

Rainbolt went back and lay down beside Shaun. The riders were out of sight now, cut off by the trees and the hills of the south-banked angle of the mountains.

Everything that Shaun had done made sense and yet Rainbolt was disturbed by some unnatural passiveness in the man that he had never seen before.

Shaun felt his partner's unrest. He said, "They won't stay long, I'm thinking."

"You're awful sure."

"I got a feeling," Shaun answered, and was silent.

Rainbolt had a feeling too, that they should leave and go up the pass a ways. They could bury the gold then and go on with the lightened calico and from the mountains make any stand they pleased.

He studied the empty space where the riders would have to appear when they left the ranch and came this way. It was a funny thing how settlers kept pushing their way into remote places in spite of Comanches and Apaches and Utes. The Hudsons were two more who had defied distance and danger to make a home in the valley.

It was an old valley. The Spanish had ranged up and down it before anyone had ever heard of Plymouth Rock. Some of them had settled here and the Indians had driven them back, time and again, to Taos or Santa Fe; or, more simply, the Indians had killed them. But pioneering was a disease that killing could not cure, and so for centuries there had always been civilization of a sort somewhere in the valley.

The Hudsons were a new kind of people.

Four years ago they hadn't been here, Shaun said. Coming across the valley, headed for the big springs where he had camped many times before, Shaun had stopped his pony suddenly and stared disgustedly, muttering something about the country going to hell.

Far ahead was a spot of green reaching out from a grove of cottonwoods against the hills. A little later Rainbolt made out the log house back in the trees. It did not look like a Mexican place. He said, "Maybe we can trade horses there."

"That would be too much good luck," Shaun said gloomily.

They went past an acre of green plants in rows. Shaun stared at the field with suspicion. "What's that stuff?"

Rainbolt had to keep looking for a long time himself before he said, "Potatoes. I think it's potatoes."

They went on into the grove of cottonwoods. John Hudson had been watching their coming. He was standing with a rifle at his side, a tall man, well built, with an air of sternness that impressed Rainbolt. It might be that he was just a trifle too handsome in his neat clothes but there was a steadiness in his manner that Rainbolt liked.

And then the woman came out of the house. Her name was Gail and she was Hudson's daughter, but Rainbolt didn't know those facts until later. She was a tall woman with honey-colored hair that was burned in streaks by the sun, and her face was darkened from the sun so that her gray eyes looked larger than they were. She had the coolest eyes that had ever looked from a woman's face at Rainbolt.

Hudson was cordial enough but still he was reserved. Shaun and Rainbolt were welcome to stay the night. "We don't see white men very often, just an officer and a few cavalrymen scouting now and then from Fort Massachusetts."

The woman stood beside her father. It looked to Rainbolt as though she wasn't sure whether she considered him and Shaun white men. Well, maybe you couldn't expect a woman to be delighted when a pair of long-whiskered buck-runners in ragged deer hide came bumping into her yard on Indian ponies just shedding their winter's hair.

Hudson told Shaun that he was sorry but he had no mounts for sale or trade. He looked the unshod Ute ponies over with a critical eye. "Perhaps some of my field hands would trade, but I sent them all out hunting yesterday."

Rainbolt looked at a dirt-roofed log building that was obviously quarters for whatever kind of crew Hudson had. There was a broken Mexican saddle on a stump near the doorway. Strings of chili peppers were hanging from the roof logs.

Shaun and Rainbolt went back in the trees to camp. They passed a corral with two big sorrel horses in it, and there was a team of California mules in another smaller corral.

"Field hands," Shaun said, and ground his teeth. "I remember people like him back in Virginia. That's where he's from. You hear him talk?"

"I knew he was southern."

Both Shaun and Rainbolt shaved. With sand they scoured some of the campfire grime and trail dust from themselves, but even then they weren't anything special in the eyes of the Hudsons.

Hudson invited them into his house for a drink. It was brandy. He did not offer them a second drink. The house made them uncomfortable; it was too well furnished for a frontier place. The logs were hewed inside and the spaces between them were plastered with white clay. There was even a board floor.

Hudson spoke of his cattle. Shaun and Rainbolt looked sidewise at each other. Shaun asked, "You're running 'em loose here?"

"Of course. They've got the whole valley and the mountains in which to find forage."

"You ain't tried to round up any of them yet?" Rainbolt asked.

"Not yet. I've been short of help. The people one can hire out here are not the most reliable in the world."

The brandy glass in Shaun's hand was a tiny, delicate thing, almost hidden by his thumb and two fingers. He put it down carefully on a table. "I'll look around," he said, and went outside.

Rainbolt got up too. He looked back from the doorway at Gail. She was standing by the fireplace, tall and cool. She watched him quietly as he left.

Shaun made a restless tour around the buildings. He stood in the trees and looked for a long time back along the way he and Rainbolt had come. The sun was going down. There was no wind on the valley and everything looked clear and lonely on the back trail. Shaun came back to Rainbolt. ". . . in which to find forage," the old man growled.

"Every man is a greenhorn once in his life, Shaun. He'll learn."

"He never will. He'll sit in there looking down his nose at the Utes when they're dragging his girl away and beating in his skull. 'The folks you hire out here ain't the most reliable in the world.'" Shaun spat and went back to the camp by the horses. Ten minutes later he was making another prowl, staring out toward the La Garitas.

When the sunset was running pale red on the Blood of Christ Mountains, Gail came from the house and stood in the yard. Rainbolt watched her for a time and then he went over to her. The woman of her made a strong appeal to Rainbolt. He had to remember that she was white and that a man, even one who had been all winter in the mountains, could not run wild on impulse.

"Is that your ma's grave back there in the trees?"

The woman gave Rainbolt a calm look. "One of the Mexicans who worked for us is buried there."

"Field hand?"

She ignored this oblique insult to her father, looking at the color on the mountains that gave them their name. In the silence glass clinked lightly on glass inside the house. Gail Hudson might not have heard that either.

"How long have you been here?" Rainbolt asked.

"Two years."

"It's a lonely life."

"That's what Lieutenant Merriam at the fort says. Do you mean it's lonely for me or you, Mr. Rainbolt?"

"For you."

She looked at Rainbolt's worn buckskins, at the ragged knife-trimmed head of thick auburn hair, at the bold planes of his face. "How long have you been here?"

"Counting everything, eight years this spring. I'm leaving for good now, me and Shaun."

Gail Hudson kept studying him. She smiled faintly. "I wouldn't bet on that. I imagine your friend back there has said the same thing a hundred times."

"Maybe he has, but this time we're both going."

Gail went back to her remoteness again, watching the blazing fire-color on the mountains.

"You've got folks back east, ain't you?" Rainbolt asked.

"My mother, yes." After a time Gail Hudson added calmly, "She was here. One day she had enough of things. She rode away alone to go home. She went home."

Under his breath Rainbolt said, "My God!" A white woman starting out from the San Luis Valley alone to cross the mountains on her way back east. Gail Hudson looked about as strong willed as her ma must have been. The thought scared Rainbolt and fascinated him at the same time.

Rainbolt stayed with her until the flames died to grayness on the sharp new mountains above the ancient lake bed. There seemed to be nothing she wanted to talk about. Rainbolt went back to the camp in the trees. Shaun was cleaning his rifle, fondling it almost absently. "We're being followed, boy."

"I saw no sign of it." Rainbolt knew better than to insult Shaun by saying that he was jumpy.

"You will." Shaun looked like an Indian as he sat stone-faced in the dusk. "That calico will hardly be able to waddle tomorrow."

Rainbolt looked at the corrals where the big mules were. "Let's show Hudson some gold and maybe —"

"I wouldn't have anything from him as a gift."

Gail was walking toward the house through the soft gloom. Rainbolt watched until she went into the house.

Shaun said, "Long winter, wasn't it, boy?"

"I wasn't thinking of that."

Shaun laughed deep inside himself. His humor was brief. He held his rifle and stared into the dusk.

"You *are* going back all the way, Shaun?"

"Said so. We'll stop a spell on the Huerfano and then we'll go back all the way."

Rainbolt did not rest well. Every time he roused to see about the horses, Shaun was gone. Sometimes he returned before Rainbolt was asleep again; but Shaun spent little of the night resting. He was as edgy as a black cat in new snow.

Once Rainbolt asked him, "You think this fellow we met on the way out of the San Juan —"

"I know. Green River runs with a pack of

wolves, McCracken and some others. You've heard me talk about McCracken. They were off somewhere when we passed their camp. Green River saw enough. I tell you, they're following us."

Sometime in early morning darkness Rainbolt slipped quickly out of his robes when he heard the muffled clop of hoofs. Shaun was already ahead of him. A few minutes later Rainbolt heard him talking in Ute to someone out beyond the cottonwoods. The answers came in Ute.

When Shaun returned to the trees, he sensed that Rainbolt was somewhere close by. "Some of Mano's young whelps out after Arapahoe hair," Shaun said.

Sliding by to make the cover of timber before dawn, Rainbolt thought. "Did they see —"

"No. They didn't come the way we did. Let's get out of here."

They ate a cold breakfast and made ready to leave. The calico almost collapsed when they put the burden of gold on the packsaddle. Maybe you could not blame Hudson for not letting them have at least one mule; but Rainbolt did not like the man anyway. At first he had looked all right, but after talking to him Rainbolt had changed his mind about John Hudson.

The house was dark and silent as they passed it. Rainbolt said something about Hudson's daughter, and Shaun grunted a comment, "You don't expect to get that kind of woman for hawk bells, do you?"

They went toward the dunes. After a short time it was evident that the ponies had not benefited much from the night's rest. When they made the barter for ponies with Mano's people they hadn't had much to barter with. After the trading Shaun had made some bitter remarks about the value of two hundred and fifty pounds of gold, all of which could not have gained them three good horses from the Utes. After a time they had to stop and let the animals rest and forage.

They were a long time reaching the dunes, but now they were here and Shaun was lying like a big lizard on the brown sand, watching for the pursuers and seemingly lost in his queer mood of the last five days.

Rainbolt slid back and went out to the horses again. Sand was packed so tightly inside his boots that he had to lie on his back and let most of it spill down his legs before he could remove the boots.

There was a curious stillness of air in the middle of the hollow, but eerie music was playing like a devil's orchestra higher up the dunes, and in the deepest bank of the cove the wind was eating a new hole. Fascinated by the swift moving of the sand, Rainbolt watched the hole grow larger.

Something dark appeared. The sand swirled around it and the dark object kept thrusting higher. Rainbolt went over to it. Close now to the bank, he felt the powerful sucking force of the wind. It was a breastplate of armor sticking there in the sand, the metal rusted to lacy fragility. It broke at the level of the sand when Rainbolt started to pull it free.

Rainbolt took the fragment over to Shaun, who stared at it as if the oldness of the armor and its mystery signified something that he feared. He licked the sand from his lips and said, "Bury it again," and his tone of voice was strange.

The lower half of the armor was coming out of the sand. Rainbolt went back to it and dug around it, lifting gently. He fitted the two sections together and held them against his chest. The man who had worn the breastplate, perhaps died with it on him somewhere in the shifting sand, had been quite small.

Rainbolt let the pieces fall back on the sand. The wind ran over the holes in the metal with a forlorn whistling sound that carried to Shaun's ears.

"Bury it!" Shaun said.

Rainbolt took the pieces of armor over to the low ridge and crushed them into the sand and the wind smoothed away the marks as he stood watching. Once more the pressure of sand inside his boots was almost enough to shut off circulation. He went back and lay down again beside Shaun.

"They've had time to reach the ranch," Shaun said. "They'll be coming. They'll have fresh horses, two of 'em at least."

"The sorrels?"

"Yes. I know McCracken."

"Let's go on up the pass and get ready for them."

"There's one man on the Huerfano you can trust — Dimasio Gondora. I know about everybody there, but Dimasio is the one you can trust."

"All right," Rainbolt said. "Let's go see him."

"Roman Aragon, you can't trust. He don't shine."

"We'll shoot Aragon and scalp him first thing we see him. Let's go."

"That's about the size of it, I guess," Shaun said, still watching the valley. "Dimasio is all right."

Rainbolt went over to the panniers. They were an awkward weight. He waited for

Shaun to help him throw them on the calico, but Shaun didn't move. "Are we going?"

"I guess." Shaun slid down from the ridge and got up. He put a sharp, inquiring look all around the hollow. "Yes, we're going. We don't want 'em to see us coming from here." He walked up on the barrier of sand to the east. He looked toward the gulch and then he turned and walked back across the hollow and kicked his moccasin against the high wall of the cove. He put his rifle down and walked over to Rainbolt. "Over there by the rifle we'll bury the gold."

"No! Not the way the wind can change things here."

Shaun drove his hand downward. "See that grass, such as it is? This hollow ain't been covered up. Right over there by the rifle we'll cache the gold, boy."

Rainbolt looked at the wind streaming sand on the high ridges. He did not trust the dunes. They were treacherous. They had held that piece of Spanish armor for no telling how long, perhaps moving it hundreds of feet from where it once had been.

Yet Shaun was right; there was vegetation underfoot to prove that this hollow was a place that had long been bare because of some vagary of the wind currents. Time was not going to have a chance to ply its changes on the gold as it had worked upon the breastplate. In a few days, at the most, Shaun and Rainbolt would be back for their treasure.

They carried the panniers over to Shaun's rifle. They dumped the sacks of gold against the toe of the bank where the sand was running laterally after it came pouring down the bank. With their hands they dug down into the coldness and buried the sacks. It was done quickly. Rainbolt picked up the panniers and stared doubtfully at the bank. It was incredible how fast the gold had disappeared.

Rainbolt heard the wind screaming its discordant music as he threw the panniers back on the calico. They led the horses in a floundering plunge up the low ridge and Rainbolt stopped to look back into the basin. Unless a man got down on his hands and knees to study sign, he would never know that they had been in the hollow.

Shaun pointed toward the lightning-blasted cottonwood. "Six hundred and ten steps from there, boy. Sight through the forks of the tree to that patch of gray rocks on the mountains. Got it?"

Rainbolt had it, but he kept sighting until he fixed a third reference point in mind, the smoke-gray deadness of a tall pine standing in direct line between the forks of the cottonwood and the gray rocks. He would not forget this place. Six hundred and ten steps.

They led the horses across the skirts of the dunes and the wind rippling on the sand covered their tracks almost as soon as they were made. When they turned up Medano Creek where the waters of the stream were soaking away into the sand, their trail did not blow over as they went. Rainbolt held his feet high and let the sand run from his boots. Watching the back trail as he rode, Shaun removed his moccasins and shook them.

They came to a place where spring floods had left sticks and pine cones and other debris spread widely over an area where the surface of the ground was cracked and broken into little brown squares upcurled at the edges. They eyed this stretch of ground keenly, knowing that underneath the dried top there would be soft dampness.

Without dismounting they both transferred to the calico, driving the other two ponies before them. The calico braced itself wearily against the weight. Its hoofs cut deeply into the softness and it left a heavy trail across the damp place. Before they were fairly started up the pass they had to travel across muddy ground beside beaver ponds. Each time they shifted to the calico.

"Very much more of this and we'll kill the horse," Rainbolt said.

"Green River can read sign like an Apache."

Before them in the trail were the marks of the Ute war party that had gone up the pass in early morning. After a time the path turned sharply away from the course of Medano Creek, twisting upward through stands of aspen where heavy leaf mold dampened the sound of the horses' feet.

"Stop here," Shaun said.

They could not see the near part of the valley. Rainbolt got down quickly with his rifle. They tied the ponies in the aspens. Shaun led the way up the side of the mountain and they came to a rocky point above the trembling trees. From here they could see across the foothills to the Hudson ranch.

Six riders were coming rapidly toward the pass. Rainbolt narrowed his eyes against the distance as he watched the dust. Two of them were lagging somewhat but the four in the lead were kicking dust in such a quickly growing stream there could be no doubt they were on untired horses.

"Hudson's sorrels and Hudson's mules," Shaun said. He turned on his back and lay looking at the sky as if, now that it was fully established, the pursuit did not matter. "Dimasio likes gold as well as any man, but still you can trust him."

"You said that twice."

"Don't forget it."

They watched from the rocky point until the riders reached the dunes. When the horsemen came out of the sandy gulch to where Shaun and Rainbolt's trail disappeared, they spread out, two of them going into the piñons, the other four riding side by side on the skirts of the dunes. No one went near the hollow.

They picked the trail up beside Medano Creek. They rode slowly, looking at the tracks in the soft crossing, and then they came full tilt for the pass.

By then Rainbolt could make out that two of the horses were indeed sorrels.

Shaun said, "Five men. That man in back is trailing a spare horse."

Rainbolt stared for a few moments longer. He could not be sure of what Shaun had said about the last man; but everything else old Shaun had said was turning out to be the truth. "This McCracken you mentioned —"

"Don't worry about him, unless he's in back of you. . . ."

They went down to the horses in long leaps.

They left the aspens and struck a steep, hard climb over rocks. The calico wanted to rest but Shaun kept lashing it. Rainbolt's pony was growing more sore-footed by the minute. Before long they would have to pick their spot and make their stand.

CHAPTER THREE

From the rocks above a small grassy pocket on the west side of Mosca Pass a thin, brown, frightened face peered out as the boy, Chico Jaramillo, listened to the scrabbling on the trail below him. More of the Black Ones, the Utes, were coming. Five of them had gone by in the morning, all of them as big as devils.

They had ridden past Chico while he lay in the trees near the old camping place of the Spanish governor who had led his army after Comanches. They were dark and deadly riders, their moccasins swinging by the winter-shaggy bellies of their ponies, their faces streaked for war, their bitter, savage eyes looking everywhere as they rode.

Two of them had laughed about something and the sound made Chico press his face close to the damp earth. For a long time he had not stirred from the place. They might have seen him. They might be waiting close at hand, grinning silently, waiting for him to show himself.

For a long time Chico did not move. There was only the deep silence of the mountains around him. The gray birds came close, bouncing like puffs of smoke as they lit in the spruce trees to look down on him, cocking their heads and showing their bright little eyes.

In time he rose and hurried away from the trail.

Except for the burro he would have kept running toward home to tell of the five — or was it ten? — enormous Utes who had tried to kill him. But the burro had escaped from Chico while he was dreaming around the camping place of the Spanish governor. The burro was from Costilla and undoubtedly it had not forgotten and would go there; for Costilla, or any other place, surely must be a better place to be than around the home of Chico's uncle, Roman Aragon.

Chico stopped running. He could not go home without the burro. He feared his uncle almost as much as he feared the Utes. This was a bad day, and all from taking his eyes from the burro for only a moment while he searched for a coin, perhaps a broken sword, or maybe a pistol that some careless soldier had left behind long ago at the camping place.

After standing by a tree for several minutes, Chico wrought courage from fear and began to look for the burro. In truth, the burro had started toward the west side of the pass, toward the great valley. It had left its tracks near the edges of rotting snowbanks and on the close-standing pines it had left gray hair from its coat where it squeezed between the rough-barked trees.

He trailed the burro for an hour, until he could see the San Luis Valley and all its vastness spread between the blue mountains. It was a very far distance to Costilla. The burro was stubborn and would keep going.

Chico worried. He did not know what to do now. In his pocket there were two tortillas which he had told himself he would eat when he found the burro. But he was not going to find the burro now. He ate the tortillas and lay down against some warm rocks in a little basin. Perhaps he could tell his uncle that the Utes had run away with the burro. He had seen them drive the burro away and he had run for a long distance, dodging through the trees and rocks until he was safe.

The Black Ones had hunted for him, but he had crawled into a hole among the rocks and they could not find him. Yes, that was a fine, brave story and it would serve.

Chico fell asleep in the warm sun.

The scrabbling sounds on the trail roused him. More Indians were coming. In truth, it was a terrible day. Chico's uncle had sent him to the mountains to see how the grass was coming along the Rito Oso, where Roman Aragon was going to hide for the summer the cows he had taken from the Hudsons, the crazy gringo who had built a house at the big springs beyond the sand dunes.

For dawdling at the camp ground of the Spanish army, and not going near the Rito Oso, and for letting the burro get away, Chico was being punished with Indians. Surely this time they would see him and chase him through the trees with their lariats. He was too scared to run. He would lie very still, like the snow rabbit with the big feet, which moved not even its eyes as it crouched in the snow.

Yet Chico was curious to see the Indians, terrible as they were. It was possible to see them and still be undetected. He scrambled up to the top of the little basin and lay between two rocks.

He could hear the heaving of the horses, the whack of a quirt or lariat, the frantic scuffling of hoofs on the rocky bed of the trail. The first rider came in sight. He was wearing a white man's hat. No, it was a white man dressed in dirty deer hide clothes. He was big and he had a fierce face with heavy bones.

Behind him was a spotted packhorse, its sides heaving under the loose panniers that hung across the crude saddle. The second man was surely an Indian, dark of face, with black hair, and a quick, tough look about him. But no, he was not a Ute either.

It was the big one who sometimes stayed all winter with Dimasio Gondora, the man called Shaun, who sang and danced and made great laughter sometimes. There was nothing happy about him now. He looked as dangerous as the Black Indians that had ridden past. Chico was afraid to call out to the men; they were angry about something.

They stopped right in front of Chico. They got down from their horses and walked back down the trail a short distance with their rifles. They stood very quietly, listening. They talked about something in low voices, growing more angry. Shaun motioned the other man back to the horses and they argued about that.

Shaun pointed down the mountain with his rifle, holding it as if it were a little stick. At last they both went down the trail and out of sight. The horses were too tired to move for a while. Long afterward it occurred to Chico that he could have crept out and taken one of the ponies and ridden home. But at the moment there was only a delicious fear in him as he waited to find out what would happen down the mountain, and he thought of none of the things that occurred to him later.

Everything was very quiet. Indians, of course, were coming up the trail. Shaun and the other man had gone back to fight them.

The heavy boom of a rifle rolled out across the mountains. Chico's mouth flew open. He craned to see down the trail. The echoes of the shot growled faintly among the peaks and then there was silence again.

Chico heard light sounds on the trail. The young man came running first, with Shaun behind him. They both looked so grim, so intent on their deadly business, that Chico was afraid to call out to them. With their heavy rifles swinging at their sides they ran to the horses and went on up the trail.

By now Chico's fascination had almost overcome his fear. He knew he should slip away but still he wished to see the Utes that the two white men had shot at. He could go home with a great tale to tell his uncle, a true tale this time, and perhaps it would be enough to make Roman Aragon forget about the lost burro. The burro that the Utes had taken.

When the sounds of Shaun and his companion began to fade, Chico grew afraid once more. Suppose the Utes came filtering through the trees, spread out wide? Then they would find him lying here. It was time to go.

But Chico had waited too long.

A tall sorrel came in sight, lathered, heaving. There was never any doubt about the rider being a white man. Chico saw the paleness of his eyes as he looked straight at the rocks. Chico saw a face without mercy, an expression without anger, and it frightened him more than his uncle's rage-twisted features ever had.

The man studied the rocks. Like the rabbit of the deep snows, Chico moved not even his eyes. The man's nose was thin, his jaw wide and tight, and his gaze was like winter coldness blowing from the mountains. He was Evil. Chico knew it instinctively. Without thinking, Chico closed his eyes, and prayed.

When he looked again his prayers had not made the man disappear, but at last the fellow was no longer looking at Chico. More riders were coming. There was a second tall sorrel. Chico knew those sorrels. The man at the big springs in the San Luis owned them. He had brought them up the Huerfano two years ago, along with mules and a herd of cattle.

Everyone had talked about the sorrels. Chico's uncle was still talking of stealing them; but the man at the big springs in the valley took much better care of them than he did his cows, which were allowed to wander freely so that anyone could steal them.

Two beautiful sorrel horses and two great mules, all of them tired. The last man, who was on a mule, had a rifle in his hands and still another in the scabbard. The leader waited only until he knew that the others were coming and then he went on up the trail.

The last man, the one with two rifles, swept a look across the rocks where Chico lay. The turning of his head revealed that one side of his face was horribly scarred. The sight was one last shock to Chico. Devils, he was sure, were loose in the mountains.

The maimed one passed. Chico had seen all that one small boy cared to see in one day. When he no longer heard any sounds on the trail, he crept out of the basin and trotted toward home. It was late. He could not use the trail. He knew he would not get home tonight but would have to huddle somewhere in the trees with the long darkness all around him.

As he ran away on skinny legs, barefooted, with his thin cotton pants flapping, he knew that no matter how exciting a story he told his uncle, Roman Aragon would not overlook the loss of the burro.

CHAPTER FOUR

Shaun had wanted to go back down the trail alone, telling Rainbolt to stay with the horses. The horses did not need any watching; they were almost dead. Rainbolt said, "We'll both go." Never before, during an emergency, had they argued about procedure, and now Rainbolt wondered about the change in Shaun.

They both went down the trail and crouched behind a shoulder of rock that commanded a turn below them. In some ways it was an ideal ambush. The pursuers would have to come around the turn below one at a time. The lower side of the trail plunged away on a steep fall into timber; the upper side ran up into tumbled rocks.

But the same conditions that made the ambush spot good also made it bad. The timber below and the rock field above offered ideal cover for flankers, and the very sharpness of the turn almost ensured that the pursuers were not going to come around it recklessly, exposing themselves in a tight line.

Rainbolt put a fresh cap on his rifle.

He was nervous. McCracken and Green

River and the others were white men, like himself.

Rainbolt murmured, "Maybe we could scare them back, hold them behind that turn without —"

"That bunch, we'll have to kill. It's part of the price of the gold."

The gold was not on the packhorse, but the pursuers' belief that it was had to be maintained. Gold was a costly possession, after all, Rainbolt thought; but it belonged to him and Shaun, others were trying to take it from them, and you had to protect what was yours.

My God! Back home this would be nothing but murder. Rainbolt had little time to moralize. They heard the riders coming. Shaun settled a little lower. Rainbolt licked his finger and used the wetness of it to wipe the dust from the front sight of his rifle.

Steel ground on rock. Shaun and Rainbolt caught a glimpse of the riders on a far turn in the timber and then the whole group was out of sight behind the shoulder of the mountain. They did not come bursting around the turn.

After several moments a man peered from around the rocky shoulder of the turn. Someone behind him said something in an impatient, urging tone. The man still hesitated. There was not much of him to see, half of his face, the side of his hat, and a rifle slanting forward.

Sprawled flat now, with his rifle bearing through the shadowy opening between two rocks, Rainbolt kept his aim full on the trail. If there was a rush he would take the second man, knowing that Shaun would take the first one. Long ago such details had been worked out and settled between them.

Again, someone behind the turn urged the first man on, but the fellow was not satisfied with the quietness ahead. He turned and said something in an angry tone to those behind him. The movement exposed a full side view of his head.

Shaun's rifle bellowed. Bitter smoke blew across Rainbolt's face. The man at the turn pitched out into the trail and Rainbolt knew that he was dead.

Shaun rolled on his side and reloaded.

Rainbolt kept watch for a flanking movement above or below the trail. No one came near the dead man.

They drew away quietly and then they ran back up the trail toward the horses. The threat of their presence was still behind. It would take a half hour, Rainbolt estimated, before the pursuers could make sure that they had withdrawn.

The sight of the empty panniers on the drooping calico gave Rainbolt an uneasy moment. A white man was dead — over nothing.

He grabbed the war rope of his pony and tugged the animal into a wobbling trot.

Even in the thin air, running up a steep trail, Shaun was faster than the ponies. He was panting and his buckskins were soaked with sweat but he knew he still had deep reserves. He was not nearly as old and used-up as he had been making himself believe. Action was like a tonic to him. If it came right down to it, he could probably outrun Rainbolt from here to the Huerfano.

He led his pony and kept whacking at the calico, which was being towed by Rainbolt's pony.

Ben Onstead, that's who it had looked like down there at the turn. Ben had always had more guts than craft. He never should have exposed himself like that, even with McCracken egging him on. It damned sure wasn't McCracken who had looked out around the turn, not that there was any lack of guts in him.

Cautiously Shaun began to wonder if things might not work out after all. If McCracken's bunch worked around the point of ambush, like they should, they would be held up quite a spell.

And then he heard them coming behind him. They had not waited. McCracken had outguessed him. It was like the crack of doom.

Shaun's strange premonitions came back doubly strong.

That piece of armor had cinched it. Somewhere in the sky, or in the deep forest, or behind a cloudy mountain, something big and unbeatable turned at an appointed time. It said, *Shaun Weymouth's stick floats that way,* and there was nothing you could do to change the pronouncement, except you didn't go into your lodge and lie down. Because you were a white man you played it out all the way.

After maybe three hundred years why had that piece of armor come to light out of the dark insides of dunes that were old beyond time? Why had the wind moved the sand from it just when Shaun Weymouth was there? It was simple; it was merely a mark of the darkly-turning process that no man could stay.

That was fate. Shaun wouldn't quarrel with it; but McCracken and his boys, instruments of fate though they might be, were still merely a pack of curs that were going to find old Shaun's hide tough chewing.

Still trotting, Shaun followed Rainbolt up the pass. It was good to feel the strength and bounce he still had in his muscles after all those years of wading cold streams, of sleeping in wet buckskin, of starving when things went wrong.

In the dark timber below he caught brief flashes of the pursuers, like a bunch of Blackfeet on the run through a dense thicket. A rifle bellowed and a bullet splatted on a rock under the calico's belly. Shaun gave a defiant whoop and lashed the packhorse around a turn.

Sure they'd shoot at the packhorse. That was good; that was evidence that they thought the gold was still on it.

It was about a half mile to the top of the pass. If the ponies didn't choke up and break before they reached the top, they would have the advantage over the bigger animals going downhill. Rainbolt could go on ahead to the Huerfano. Shaun would stay behind and do what must be done.

Rainbolt led his pony up a steep pitch. The horses were a liability now. They would be better off to cut loose from them and go on foot into the timber; but they had to carry out the deception with the calico.

Rainbolt had enough of running away. He

stopped and turned toward Shaun. "Let's fight 'em off!"

Shaun waved his rifle toward the bare mountain on their right. He looked downhill into the timber. It was a poor place for an ambush and he didn't have to say it. He motioned Rainbolt on.

The eyes of the ponies were glazed with strain, their muzzles gray with foam. They looked close to dying, but the mustang toughness was in their bones and they had lived on abuse since the first Ute leaped on their backs. They bunched their hind quarters for another staggering surge up the mountain.

The bare hillside expanded, rock studded, holding in its hollows banks of snow. On the left the timber fell farther below. A chill wind was slicing through the wide notch in the mountains. Looking back across his shoulder as he trotted, Rainbolt suddenly realized that the sun was setting.

The top of the pass was always one steep pitch beyond the one that appeared to be the summit. Rainbolt's horse stopped so suddenly that the war rope twisted Rainbolt sidewise and threw him to his knees. The pony's head was down. It stood on widespread feet, swaying.

Rainbolt took only a brief look at it before

he cut his plunder sack loose from behind the saddle and tossed it back to Shaun, who shoved it into the panniers on the calico. Rainbolt grabbed the lead rope of the packhorse.

Back down the trail they heard the crash of steel on rock and the smack of a whip as a rider urged his mount on. Rainbolt and Shaun went around the stricken pony, leaving it standing in the trail.

The summit of the pass came unexpectedly. The ponies went across the saddle at a wobbling trot. Shaun panted, "Stay with the right-hand forks."

He ran to the side and flung himself down where three stunted spruce trees made a clump. Rainbolt trotted on ahead with the horses, taking them to cover below the break of the saddle. Presently he returned, running low, off the left of Shaun. There was no cover over that way, except a discolored drift of snow.

The top of the pass here was a poor place for an ambush, and that was why Shaun had selected it. The first place had been good, but it had not fooled McCracken; maybe he would make his blunder here.

Shaun saw Rainbolt duck in behind the snowbank.

The clatter of the pursuers' horses

sounded under the crest, but no riders came up boldly to rush across the saddle. They had stopped below the last steep pitch. Only the noise of the wind and his own breathing came to Shaun.

Before long Shaun grew uneasy. Some of them must be working around below the hill, slicing through the timber on his right. There were four of them left. If he could get McCracken, the chances were that the other three would lose a lot of their desire to see old Shaun Weymouth at close range.

Green River would, for one. He was no coward, but like an Indian, he sized up chances and never took the short side when he could help it. Shaun had done the same thing a hundred times himself and he had lived for thirty years in a country where some men went under during their first summer out from the settlements.

But Shaun had been outguessed again. He had played it first one way and then the other, and both times McCracken was ahead of him. Well, that was the way the thing had been arranged somewhere, but it was still enraging to have a white man beat you at your own game.

Knowing McCracken, Shaun was sure they were drifting around to the right. There might be one man with the horses, maybe not even one. Shaun considered the prospects of a wild, quick stroke to get their horses. The thought appealed to the Indian side of him; but the other part of his nature made the idea retreat before a cold feeling of inevitability: Whatever he did was likely to be wrong. It could be that McCracken had set a trap of his own at the horses.

No matter how it was shaping up, this was no place to lie idly after the ambush had misfired. Shaun signaled Rainbolt to go back to the horses and continue the flight. Rainbolt did not move until Shaun himself started falling back.

Instead of going all the way to the horses, Shaun swung off to the right to look down into the timber. Silent as smoke he slipped from one tree to another. Down in the gloomy timber on the steep hill the tops of the trees were moving slowly in the wind. Shaun crouched at the edge of the break.

He saw the flicker of motion between two spruces as a man went from one to another. Shaun settled lower, raising his rifle. The man made another advance, indistinct, just a leap across space from one tree to the next. Now the line of his movement was settled in Shaun's mind. He covered the right side of the next gap.

Too late he saw the movement of boughs. A rifle slammed from the trees below and the ball cut through the flesh of Shaun's left arm as he was shifting aim. The impact threw his rifle out of line and he knew it was too late to shoot, for by then the man would be behind the trunk of a tree.

From the snowbank came the hard smack of Rainbolt's rifle, and then Shaun heard the racketing of hoofs. He ran back from the break of the hill. A sorrel horse was sidling out in the open, stepping away nervously from the motionless bundle of a man lying on the ground.

Shaun motioned for Rainbolt to go back to the horses. Rainbolt obeyed, reloading as he ran, and Shaun covered the falling back. They met at the ponies.

"How many started across?" Shaun asked.

"Two."

It was a pitching drop to the heavy timber below. The calico began to take shortcuts on the turns and as it did it took one too many and fouled the tow rope around a dead tree. The slack took up and threw the calico sidewise and almost upset Rainbolt.

Shaun cut the rope with a quick stroke of his knife.

They hazed the packhorse ahead of them

and went twisting on down the pass.

And soon the sounds of pursuit came on behind them.

McCracken would never give up, Shaun knew.

CHAPTER FIVE

Now it was dusk and before long it would be dark. From the shadows of tumbled rocks Frank McCracken looked two hundred yards down the hill where the trail lay starkly exposed for fifty yards or more across a blowout of white quartz. That part of the trail was the far side of a narrow horseshoe that ran around the head of a canyon. Dense timber covered the near side of the turn, and at the bend there was a waterfall, unseen, but sending up its booming noise.

Standing at the shoulder of a mule, Sam Guthrie, sometimes trader and more often thief, said, "Maybe they got across already."

"They couldn't have," McCracken said. "We've been crowding them too close."

Green River said nothing. He knew Shaun Weymouth was the kind of man who would lie out in that heavy timber and let them pass, and then explode at their backs like seven Blackfoot Indians. Now that dark was coming, Green River had had about enough of Shaun Weymouth.

McCracken said calmly, "They're in the timber."

"Hard to do anything there, with only

three of us," Guthrie said. He was a tall man with a stoop to his shoulders. His whiskers made a light brushing noise on the shoulder of his buckskin shirt as he turned his head to study the black pools of timber.

"We'll do it," McCracken said. "Against that light rock we can pick off the calico if they make their break. We'll wait it out."

"If they don't cross tonight?" Green River asked.

"We'll go in on foot when it's dark."

Green River looked at the sky. "Ain't going to be real dark any time tonight. Suppose they take out through the timber right there at the falls?"

"They can't get horses through. That timber is tangled like hair on a shedding buffalo." They might take part of the gold and make their way out on foot through the lodgepole, McCracken knew, but he doubted that Shaun would do so. Shaun Weymouth was as stubborn as a grizzly, and more dangerous when cornered. He wasn't going to give up anything unless you took it from him.

The devil was walking beside him today. McCracken had had two fair shots at him, one there on top of the pass that should have ended it, and another long running try that any man might have missed.

"Settle down," McCracken said. "We'll wait."

The noise of the falls worried Rainbolt. He couldn't listen to the night. Here in the heavy timber the trail was a ghostly streak. You could feel your way by watching the light break at the tops of the trees ahead but if you had to go out at a fast clip to rush across the pale rock he had seen from the high switchback, you would have to let the ponies run free.

They had been held up here just by the margin of a minute or two. Once around the white rock, you had a fair run to the Huerfano, Shaun had said. But they hadn't made it quickly enough. The crash of rolling rocks on the hill had warned them that McCracken and his men were in position above them.

Now it was an ice-cold game of waiting, and Rainbolt didn't know what Shaun was thinking. Shaun had gone back around the falls. Rainbolt stood with his rifle across his thighs, trying to hear any sound that was different from the steady thrumming of the water. The ponies drowsed on their feet.

Shaun's arrival was something sensed, rather than seen or heard. The deep mat of pine needles gave back no noise. One moment there was the black channel of the trees and a moment later something was coming. From quite close Shaun said in a normal voice, "They're up on the hill."

"How's the timber back of us?"

"No good."

"If we left the horses, they'd have to think we took the gold and went on foot."

"McCracken knows me better than that," Shaun said. "He'll backtrack to that gold sure as hell if we don't get the packhorse all the way to the Huerfano."

"All right then, let's take it. I'm ready."

After a time Shaun said, "There's going to be a moon. We won't gain by waiting."

They led the ponies quietly to the edge of the trees where the passage across white rock began. There was too much light out there. Rainbolt peered around a tree at the high trail. Everything up there was in shadow, great rocks screened by pines.

"I'll lead off with the dun," Rainbolt said.

"Don't worry about the calico. I'll see he gets there."

"You coming?"

Shaun hesitated just a fraction. "I'll be along. When you make the turn, keep going. If I'm not right behind you, I'll catch you before you get to Dimasio's place."

"What's been riding you, Shaun?"

"Nothing. You set?"

"Ready."

Rainbolt was on the bright quartz, running, hauling on the war rope. The pony came stiffly at first. He saw the gushes of flame on the high trail and heard the crashing of rifles.

A bullet struck the pony and it went down with a sodden thump, jerking the war rope from Rainbolt's grip. Lying on its side it lashed the trail with its feet and rocks went cracking into the canyon. The calico came on a moment later. Shaun was yelling at it, lashing it. It went to its knees trying to jump the fallen horse.

On the high trail a rifle threw flame. The pony gained its balance with a grunting lurch and came bolting into Rainbolt. He caught a crosstree of the saddle with one hand as the animal crowded past and was dragged along with his feet bouncing from the wall. He heard Shaun fire. And then the pony skidded around the turn and ran into the timber.

Half running, half dragged, with his rifle in one hand, Rainbolt clung to the crosstree and tried to leap astride the horse. He was on the left side of the pony, the wrong side from which to mount an Indian horse. He made another effort to go up and the pony heaved away from him.

Rainbolt's last memory was hitting something hard that tore his rifle from his hand.

He heard a shot that seemed quite close, but when the echoes ran, he knew that it was up the trail some distance. He was lying in the bushes at the foot of a tree and he knew then that he had run headlong into the tree as the calico surged wildly down the trail.

Rainbolt crawled on hands and knees, casting around for his rifle. He found it some distance from where he had been lying. He ran his hand over the lock. It seemed to be all right, but when he grasped the stock, sharp splinters bit into his palm. The stock came completely loose as he was fumbling over it to determine the extent of damage.

He staggered when he rose. He could feel blood running down his face, dripping from his chin. His chest was a great dull ache. He had lost all sense of time.

He stumbled back up the trail. It was much farther than he remembered to the turn at the white cliff. From the deep shadows he peered around the turn. He thought he heard a horse stamp up on the high trail, but he could not be sure because of the booming of the falls. Over there in the timber where he had started his run, there was only blackness where the white rock ended and the trees began.

Shaun must be over by the falls, holding the back trail, waiting for McCracken; and then again he might have come across soon after Rainbolt and gone on down the trail, trusting the racket of the calico to lead him, thinking all the time that Rainbolt was with it. In the dense timber he could have passed Rainbolt while he was lying unconscious.

In any event, the packhorse was the main issue. It had to go to the Huerfano with the appearance of bearing gold. Rainbolt started away and then he hesitated. If Shaun got killed, then the gold in the dunes was all Rainbolt's. How much of that reasoning had unconsciously affected Rainbolt's decision to go on? He shrugged the thought away. Shaun knew how to take care of himself; Shaun was not going to get himself killed.

Rainbolt went on down the trail.

From the high switchback McCracken stared down at the quartz blowout. Things had gone sour. Shaun Weymouth was a crafty old devil, as elusive as a speeding white wolf. McCracken had outfigured him twice, but now how were things stacked up?

There was a dead pony down on the trail,

but McCracken was not sure that it was the packhorse. One man had got across. The two of them might have crossed during their first rush, when McCracken's eyes were confused by rifle flashes on both sides of him.

Minutes ago Green River had fired again, swearing afterward that he had seen a shadow creeping out from the trees toward the pale crossing. McCracken had seen no shadow, and he knew that Green River was always jumpy after dark. Maybe Shaun had gone across and maybe he had not.

"You're sure you saw him edge out of the timber a minute ago?" McCracken asked.

"I saw somebody," Green River answered.

"If it's Shaun, he's wounded. I know I got one into him there on top of the pass."

"Yeah." Green River was doubtful. "I know for sure that his partner did worse than that for Sandy Parker on top of the pass."

"Sandy was paid for long ago," McCracken said. He stepped away from the horses. "We'll go down on foot."

Sam Guthrie said, "If that's the packhorse, they won't be far from it."

"That's right." McCracken's voice was cool and pleasant. "I'll lead the way."

Green River put his rifle back into the sack and drew his pistol.

They kept intervals between them as they

crept down the trail. The roaring of the falls came closer. When they turned the last switchback and entered the timber, they were on deep humus and they could not hear each other five feet away.

Green River was in the middle. It was not to his liking. He thought he was as good as the next man when it came to stalking an enemy in dead-soft darkness, but he always wanted room to drive in quickly or pull out. Guthrie had jockeyed him out of last position and Green River thought it might have been because Guthrie had made hints at times about Green River not liking to fight in the dark.

They were coming close to the horseshoe, where the creek crossed the trail and plunged into the canyon. Green River caught brief glimpses of the water splashing. All at once he sensed something wrong ahead He took several long, swift strides, feeling forward with his left hand. They hadn't been that far apart before. McCracken wasn't there. He had stepped off the trail and let them pass him.

The only thing surprising about it was that Green River hadn't beat him to the idea. Both of them had let Guthrie and Sandy Parker take the brunt of things before; it was only common sense to let a man do so when he had more dumb courage than brains.

Green River took two more long strides and stepped off to the right of the trail himself. His leggings rustled against brush but the sound of the water covered the noise a few feet away. Moments later, Guthrie came by, passing so close that Green River heard the tiny scratch of his moccasins on the trail.

By craning out from the tree where he was standing Green River could see across the narrow canyon. He kept studying the dead horse, not centering his vision directly on what he wanted to see, but letting the slow sweep of his vision bear in from the sides of his eyes.

There were no panniers on the dead pony.

The one that had gone crashing down the trail when Shaun's partner escaped was the right one. The whole thing was probably ruined now. The packhorse and one man had got away, and they had such a start that it would be impossible to overtake them before they reached the Huerfano, where Shaun had strong friends.

Green River rubbed the tingling nerves on the maimed side of his face. That calico had been near swaybacked from the loot it was carrying! He had not quite given up yet; he would wait to see how Guthrie came out. Shaun might be wounded, as McCracken had claimed, but a wounded grizzly was the worst kind to stir from the bushes.

Green River waited. The dark oppressed him.

Shaun was not disabled, but now that he had been sitting still so long, his left arm was stiff from the gash of McCracken's lead.

He was sitting on a log close by the trail, in the darkest part of the horseshoe. A heavy bladed knife rested on his thigh. One moccasin was holding down the end of a long stick slanting up from a rock just ahead of Shaun's toes. The stick was Shaun's antenna, a feeler across the trail. No one could pass without running into it. On his left the stream was rushing toward the falls, its splashing almost lost in the greater sound of the water thundering into a pool in the canyon.

A man would hear the stream and know he had to cross it and have just a fraction of his mind distracted by the thought, and just about then he would nudge against the stick in the trail.

Shaun hoped it would be McCracken.

That something was near him was a sensing deeper than anything he had learned from Indians or from nights alone in the mountains. Something primordial that long security has dulled in average men told

Shaun that someone was close to him; and then on the heavy dampness swirling up from the falls he caught the stale odor of tobacco smoke, of human perspiration, the unpleasant odor of another white man.

The knife lifted from Shaun's thigh. He held it with the edge up. He could sense the other man's hesitation about the stream ahead. The natural place for an ambush was on the other side. Men have always put streams of any size between them and their enemies. This unseen man, or maybe there were more than one, would be thinking that he would betray himself crossing the water in the dark.

Shaun felt the stick slide under his moccasin. His right foot was back, toed solidly against the ground. The only sound as he made his swift rise was the small cracking sound of his knee joint as he moved.

His first knife stroke was too low. It struck and turned on heavy bone. The man grunted like an animal. Shaun made another swift, uprising arc with the knife. That one was guided by the startled sound the man had made. The hilt of the knife smacked against muscle. Shaun ripped the blade upward with his wrist stiff. In the same instant something iron hard crashed against the side of his head and he heard a shot that seemed to have exploded in his brain.

Shaun fell with the enemy he had killed.

Three other men heard the pistol shot. Rainbolt was kneeling in an aspen park where the trail branched. The noise of the pistol came distantly. Shaun carried a pistol but he seldom used it; a gun was his weapon. That was all, the one shot. Rainbolt stared back toward the black timber above the aspen thickets.

They should have stayed together, packhorse or no packhorse; but Shaun's entire action had been based on the ruse of taking the packhorse clear to the Huerfano. . . .

Rainbolt went on across the park, searching for the trail.

Green River was watching the ghostly strike of pale light on the dead pony across the canyon when the sound of Guthrie's big-charged pistol rocked the night. It was Sam Guthrie's pistol, no doubt about it.

Green River waited. If Guthrie had won he would call out. There was only silence except for the sound of the water. Green River didn't have to wait long to know that Guthrie was dead. A man was a fool to stalk old Shaun in the dark; even the Crows had never had much luck stealing horses from him. At five to two the chances had been good, but they had diminished all the way across the pass, until now they weren't worth a damn.

If it was the packhorse over there, then things would be different; a man could take long chances then.

Green River waited five minutes. He went back down the trail, calling softly to McCracken. There was no answer. Green River went back to the horses. Up there his position was much better; it would be difficult for anyone to come creeping in on him. But even then, after an hour of waiting, shadows moved and the silence built up its pressure.

McCracken was not going in to make his try, or else he had made it and lost. Green River had waited long enough. He took the four animals and started back across the pass. The weight of gold the calico had carried grew larger in his mind the farther he rode from it. Yet, two fine horses and two sound mules made a fair haul, and Green River was getting out with no holes in his hide.

Under cold starlight on top of the pass he stopped to take Sandy Parker's weapons and powder supply.

When the pistol shot came, McCracken

was working his way among close-standing trees some distance off the trail. He positioned the sound as about twenty-five yards ahead and down the hill.

McCracken waited and after a time he knew that Guthrie had failed. Green River would most likely run out now. He might have been close to the ambush, but McCracken was sure Green River had held back enough to run or go in, depending on circumstances. The silence said that he had run.

Let it be so. McCracken was going all the way. If that was the packhorse under the white cliff, both Shaun and his partner would be somewhere close. If it was not the calico McCracken was still in the game. He would go to the Huerfano and a heap farther if he had to; but when it all wound up, McCracken would have the gold.

Quite slowly he worked his way through the trees, crawling when he had to. By the time the moon came up he would have his own ambush set somewhere beside the trail beyond the point of the cliff.

CHAPTER SIX

Shaun Weymouth was sure he was dead. He had convinced himself that he was going to die somewhere between the dunes and the Huerfano. Somewhere close a great spirit dance was going on. The drums pounded with painful regularity. After a spell of see-sawing back and forth between a misty dream world and small facts of reality that began to grow larger, Shaun felt doubts about the long sleep.

He moved a little. He was dully uncomfortable and sick in some way he could not understand. There were pine needles pressed against his face. His back was bent in a manner that strained the muscles and his head was full of pain.

When a man went under he ought to be laid out in a comfortable position, at least. It came gradually to Shaun that he was not dead at all. The first real proof of it was the sound of water, and then everything started to come back. He groped weakly for his knife. It was gone. Full consciousness came through with a rush.

He was lying with his knees across a man's legs, and that had put a kink in his back. If he could feel pain he was all right, although there must be a bullet in him somewhere.

He rolled over on his back. His head bumped the spongy trail and it felt like a crack against solid rock. Everything came clear. The man had come up the trail and Shaun remembered getting him and the necessity of whirling to meet the threat of a second enemy; and then he had been shot.

He felt the side of his head. It was swollen and sticky. He had not been shot after all. The man had slammed him in the head with a heavy pistol and it had fired at the same time.

Convinced now that he was not seriously injured, Shaun recovered both his fatalism and his instincts to fight off danger. There were still two men against him. He found his knife and whipped it as one would throw water from his hand. On hands and knees he crouched in the trail feeling out the night, waiting. For a time that was all he could do, because when he tried to rise his head betrayed him and made him sink back to the ground once more.

They might have got past him while he was lying unconscious. Maybe they were pressing Rainbolt hard by now. But when Shaun began to think clearly instead of feeling his way, he knew that McCracken had not passed on this trail. McCracken would never have passed this place without making sure that Shaun was dead.

High up on the trail Shaun thought he heard the faint sound of horses, but the waterfall worked against him and he was not sure. When he got to his feet he felt his age and he felt aches in his bones that had not been there before. When he found his rifle, the cold, heavy barrel gave him back some of his assurance.

Somewhere in the dense lodgepole thickets there might have been the sound of a limb stub snapping, but once more the waterfall confused him. McCracken knew this mountain. He would not try to force horses through the lodgepole at night, Shaun was certain. It could be that one of them was trying to circle around and reach the trail beyond the cliff, while the other waited on the hill to get a shot at Shaun if he started across the white rock.

The ambush had gained all that Shaun could extract from it. It was time to move.

The full moon that had not yet risen high enough to shine down on the horseshoe was making a frosty glow on the top of the mountains when Shaun went to the beginning of the white rock. This time he was more careful about peering toward the high trail. The last time he had stepped out boldly and someone up there had sent a rifle bullet within a foot of him.

He ran across the face of the cliff. No shot came and that made him distrust the situation. Now he was not sure where his last two enemies were.

It occurred to him that they might have seen him and let him go, so that he would think they had given up. For a while Shaun lay at the turn beyond the white rocks, then got up and went on down the trail; he had to be sure he was keeping between pursuit and Rainbolt.

He remembered how his knee had popped when he rose from the log. It was hell when a man's bones began to creak. Some unseen spirit must keep track of such things and say *There's one who's old enough to die anyway. Mark him off.*

In a way Shaun Weymouth was feeling sorry for himself, regretting the days of strength and certainty that had flowed away so swiftly from the time he first went up the Missouri, a gangling kid eager to bite great chunks out of each new day.

Shaun strode down the trail. He didn't feel strong enough to run, but he knew a good place where the aspen thickets made an ideal spot for one last ambush.

★ ★ ★

Shortly after sunrise Rainbolt found the calico cropping grass in a meadow beside a brawling creek. He eyed the pony warily. Half dead yesterday while coming up the pass, the tough little brute had recuperated enough last night to run like the devil. The pony raised its head and watched Rainbolt as he approached.

Rainbolt kept talking in Ute as he walked in. The pony started to twist away and then it stopped, turning to face the man. Rainbolt was surprised that he could get close enough and snatch the frayed end of the war rope. After that the horse went back to cropping grass.

The Huerfano was close at hand, a long valley with small green fields showing beside the river. Once more Rainbolt gave thought to going back to Shaun. Or he could pull off the trail and wait. But Shaun might come to the valley on trails that Rainbolt did not know about.

Rainbolt lashed his robe and plunder sack on top of the crosstrees of the saddle. He put smooth rocks from the stream into the panniers until they gave at least some semblance of the load the calico had packed to the dunes. Some of the rocks clacked together as he started away, so he stopped and padded the load with handfuls of grass.

Later, close to the head of the valley, Rainbolt came upon a Mexican boy asleep in the sun beside the trail. The lad's clothes were ragged and torn and there were marks across his face as if he had fled headlong through heavy brush. He was not over fourteen, Rainbolt guessed, a thin, brown-faced boy sleeping as if utterly exhausted. His feet were bare, big in proportion to the rest of his size. Protective calluses were thick on them.

Sound asleep so early in the morning? It was not far to the valley where the boy undoubtedly belonged.

Rainbolt grinned. He began to talk in Ute, changing his voice to make it seem that several Indians were present. He saw the boy's eyelids move and then the youth leaped up with an expression of terror pinching his features and started to run. He stopped when he heard Rainbolt's laughter, but even then the boy was so scared that Rainbolt was ashamed of the trick.

He spoke in frontier Spanish. "What are you called, boy?"

The boy stood trembling, looking up the trail. His control came back gradually. "Chico."

"Where do I find the house of Dimasio Gondora?"

Chico pointed toward the valley.

"It is a long valley."

Curiosity was overcoming the boy's fear. He explained where Gondora lived and Rainbolt was at once lost in a maze of Mexican names. He shook his head. "You will take me there?"

Chico nodded eagerly. When he started to walk, Rainbolt saw how cruelly he limped. They went down the trail together and the boy seemed happy to have company.

"What were you doing sleeping beside the trail?"

Rainbolt saw fear come to Chico's face. "I was looking for a burro. Yesterday I lost him on the mountain and so I searched all night for him. I saw the Indians and I saw —" The boy stopped quickly.

"And bears?" Rainbolt grinned. "You saw bears also?"

"No, I saw no bears." Chico glanced sidewise at Rainbolt.

After a time, seeing how the boy was limping more and more, Rainbolt thought it likely that he *had* lost his burro and wandered on the mountain during the night. Rainbolt stopped the pony. "You'd better ride."

Rather than have Chico scramble against the sides of the panniers, feeling what was in them, Rainbolt took him under the arms and swung him up astride the robe. It was a high seat, the pannier flaps were tied, and the boy's legs did not hang down far enough for his feet to bump against the rocks in the bottom of the panniers. Rainbolt was still protecting gold that was not there.

"What will your father say about losing the burro?"

"It is my uncle. He will beat me."

Probably needed a good licking, Rainbolt thought.

They came to a grassy place where a sullen old man was sitting on a rock with a rifle, guarding a herd of goats. He nodded when Rainbolt greeted him. He turned his head slowly to watch the man and boy out of sight. Farther on they passed small flocks of sheep watched by small boys. Two of the youths shouted at Chico in such quick Spanish that Rainbolt did not catch the meaning. Chico hung his head.

"What do they say, Chico?"

"That I have lost my uncle's burro and will be beat."

They came to small fields of corn and squash. Full summer's warmth was in the air here in the low valley. Close to the creek, against the rocks, adobe houses began to appear, hard baked and squalid appearing.

Mexicans peered curiously at the pair passing with the calico.

Rainbolt did not like the Huerfano the first time he saw it. The inhabitants were too indrawn and watchful. Living close to passes where warring tribes of Indians passed back and forth all summer, with their meager livelihood continually exposed to raids, it was no wonder these people were quiet and observing, but Rainbolt still did not like the Huerfano.

They approached an adobe with a litter of pens and corrals behind it and goats peering from the doorway. Someone Rainbolt did not see shouted Chico's name. A man came striding from the house and kicked the goats aside. He stood in the yard, waiting for Rainbolt to come to him.

His face was flat and broad. His eyes were small, nested in cruelty. He was wearing buckskin pants that hung well above his ankles. Great silver spurs were strapped to his bare feet. Naked above the waist except for a leather vest that hung open and sweat-limp across a deep, brown, hairless chest, the man stood poised in anger. A mass of black curly hair hung below his ears.

Rainbolt glanced at Chico and saw that the boy was terrified.

Without warning the man in the yard ripped out a string of violent questions in

Spanish. Rainbolt did not like his tone, his attitude, and he could not follow the questions. He shifted his broken rifle lightly and from the edge of his eye he saw two men appear from somewhere in the corrals. They lounged against the rails, watching him.

The man spun out another angry question. Rainbolt spoke in Ute. "Your tongue is too long." He saw that the Mexican understood the language and he saw the deep glint of hatred in the fellow's eyes.

Chico had dismounted. He stood with one hand on a pannier, as if afraid to get far from the security of the horse. Speaking slowly in Spanish, he explained, "He is my uncle, Roman Aragon. He asks where you have been with me."

"Tell him — Never mind." Rainbolt used sign language then to explain that he had found the boy asleep beside the trail a few miles away. Aragon understood that language too. He was no settlement Mexican, hard bound to a tough existence in the valley. There were no fields around his house, and his were the first corrals of any size Rainbolt had seen. Aragon looked like a man who had ranged the mountains. He had more arrogance than an Indian in his own camp.

"I look for the home of Dimasio Gondora," Rainbolt said. He saw just a flick of caution in Aragon's expression.

"Look then."

Rainbolt glanced at the men at the corral. His bony face hardened. "Where is his house?"

Aragon stared back with a sneer. The boy Chico said, "I will go —" then wilted and was silent when his uncle looked at him.

Rainbolt hefted his rifle and led the calico on. He kept watching across his shoulder. Aragon walked over to Chico and knocked him five feet backward into the dust with a full sweep of his hand. He was raging at Chico when Rainbolt turned away.

For the first time Rainbolt understood the boy's fear and was sorry for him; but it was none of his affair. If you wanted to see kids screamed at and knocked endwise, all you had to do was to approach civilization anywhere.

Rainbolt went on down the valley. With half an eye he could see that he was no welcome visitor. He came to a cluster of houses near the biggest patch of cultivated ground he had seen so far. It looked like a good place to inquire for Dimasio Gondora. Women were making meal at a table under cottonwood trees.

Three of them had a strong Apache look in their features.

The fourth was younger and much taller than the others. At first glance Rainbolt thought that she was pure Indian, one of the high plains tribes, but there was a fineness in her facial bones that changed his mind: she was probably part Spanish.

All the women stared at him in silence. He kept his eyes on the young one. Her hair was Indian black, her eyes wide-spaced and straight. The dresses of the others were shapeless. Hers was trim and tight. Rainbolt looked at her boldly. She gave him back an even expression that told him nothing.

"I look for the house of Dimasio Gondora."

The women giggled. Rainbolt did not know whether it was because of the quaintness of his Spanish or the fact that he had forgotten them and was watching the young woman. No one answered him.

The young woman rose slowly from the table and started toward the group of houses, placed around a quadrangle like the buildings of a small fort. Rainbolt watched her going.

The women giggled again and two of them made swift remarks that set them all to laughing. They were no different from a group of Indian crones gossiping as they scraped a buffalo hide, except that Rainbolt could not follow their conversation. He ignored them and watched the young woman.

She made straight tracks as she went across the yard in her moccasins, a graceful woman who did not exaggerate the natural swing of her hips and thighs. Rainbolt tried to remember when he had seen another woman like her, and decided it had been at a Cheyenne camp in Bayou Salade two years ago.

She was not yet to the open end of the quadrangle when a deep voice boomed from inside. "Who asks for Dimasio Gondora? Who comes?"

The woman said something in a low voice. She turned and came back to the table. For a moment she gave Rainbolt quiet appraisal and then she resumed her work with the others.

Rainbolt led his horse toward the houses. A man just pulling on short cotton trousers stepped out into the sunshine. He was so small that Rainbolt could have tossed him over a tall horse without effort. His hair was snow-white above his wrinkled brown face. Rising from his beaded moccasins, his legs were like two bows faced away from each other. Even the looseness of his shapeless trousers could not hide the fact that he was a bandy-legged little man who looked as if he had spent much of his life on horses with barrels so big that he had deformed his legs trying to stay on.

"I am Dimasio Gondora. Who comes?"

The strike of Gondora's eyes changed Rainbolt's first startled impression of the man. The whole character of Gondora was in the commanding stab of his gaze, a stare as fierce as the look of an angry Piegan.

"I am a friend of Shaun Weymouth," Rainbolt said. He pointed toward the mountains. "He is coming."

Gondora studied the panniers. He looked Rainbolt over carefully, studying his swollen face, the way he held his broken rifle. "Yes, perhaps you are a friend of Shaun Weymouth." The slurring of the last name so changed the sound of it that Rainbolt would not have recognized it had he not known who Gondora was talking about.

"My house is yours." Gondora began to give orders to people Rainbolt could not see. Three men came from the buildings and went toward the calico.

"I'll do it!" Rainbolt said. He took the panniers off alone and carried them into the room where one of the men directed him. The others brought the rest of his gear to him. Gondora waved his helpers away.

"Shaun is coming?"

Rainbolt nodded. "Soon." If Shaun hadn't fallen into bad trouble, he should be here now.

"He will come, that one." Gondora looked at the panniers in the corner of the room. "Gold?"

Rainbolt nodded. "Mine and Shaun's."

"Here it is safe. Here in the house of Dimasio Gondora it is quite safe."

"Shaun said that this would be so." Rainbolt did not wish to question Gondora's honesty. He was a friend of Shaun's. Those panniers held nothing but rocks and yet he was still fretting over them as if they contained a fortune. Gondora sensed his worry and did not suggest that he leave the room. One of the old women brought water and food.

After he had eaten, Rainbolt considered going back to see about Shaun.

"I have sent men to look. He will come," Gondora said.

"I'll wait a while." Rainbolt did not want to expose the panniers again and neither did he wish to leave them to be pried into. "Who is the young woman I saw outside?"

"Paisano."

"She is of your family?"

"My sons and nephews took her from the Utes when she was a child, small and skinny.

She was like a *paisano* and so she is called that."

Paisano, road runner, a tough, scrawny bird. She was not like that now.

Gondora watched Rainbolt with an amused expression.

"Blackfoot or Cheyenne?"

Gondora shrugged. "Perhaps Cheyenne and Spanish. Who knows? She was very small when she came here."

"Whose woman is she?"

Gondora smiled. "Always that is asked. She is no man's woman." He went to the doorway. "Rest. I will tell you when Shaun arrives."

Rainbolt lay down on the floor with his head against the panniers. He was nagged by the thought that he should not put full trust in Gondora and should himself go back to find Shaun; and almost at once another thought came like a snake from a crevice: Maybe Shaun was dead and the gold in the dunes was all Rainbolt's.

He fought against the thought. It was not his own, it had come from nothing in his conscious mind. For a long time he was tense and then he began to doze. The last sound he remembered was the laughter of the women outside.

CHAPTER SEVEN

Until after sunup Shaun watched from the aspens a park where the Huerfano trail crossed boggy ground. He felt it unlikely that the two survivors from yesterday's chase would step into another trap, but he would take no chances.

Sun filtered through the pale green leaves and warmed him. His tired muscles relaxed. Considering everything, he felt pretty good. He had pried up hell with one of the toughest bunches of renegades in the mountains, outrun them and outfought them.

Maybe they hadn't given up. They might have gone around Shaun and on to the valley.

But they would not win anything from old Dimasio. Rainbolt would be at his house by now. For the time, at least, McCracken was badly licked.

Still, Shaun held stubbornly to his feeling of fatalism although it was cracked with doubts. Everything had pointed to his dying and yet he was still alive. But he could not trust his doubts too far. Many a good man had gone through what seemed the worst, only to be picked off just when he thought he was safe. Shaun still had a good chance of getting killed.

The mystic feeling would be dissolved, he knew, once he reached the Huerfano. That would be the end of it and from then on he would be starting all over again. Shaun had no desire for death. He had fought against it all his life and he would go on fighting to stay alive and whole; but still it seemed that he was cheating fate and he was suspicious of his success so far.

Now that Rainbolt had surely gotten through, Shaun was in no hurry. Deliberately he settled the sound side of his head against his arms and went to sleep. He woke instantly when a mule-eared buck started to cross the bog. Shaun watched its actions. The buck was in no hurry either; it had not been run out of its bed in a thicket. Its sprouting horns were heavy with velvet. The buck was merely wandering around in daylight.

Shaun went back to dozing. Along about noon he would get up and make his way slowly to the valley. Then, if he made it, the spell would be broken. . . .

The voice roused Rainbolt. It was a warm and musical sound and yet there seemed to be a threat in it. The room where he lay was in half gloom; someone had closed the door. Light was coming through a narrow window in the thick adobe.

Quickly Rainbolt felt the panniers to make sure they were still at his head. He took his pistol and got up, going far enough toward the window until he could see outside. A man was standing in the yard with a rifle in his arms, a trapper by his looks. He was saying in slow Spanish, "Four of them, Gondora, four of Señor Hudson's fine big cows with calves. Whoever stole them might have passed this way."

"I have not seen them."

Rainbolt leaned sidewise until he could see Gondora standing in the yard, and beyond him the women watching silently from the table under the cottonwoods. Gondora was unarmed. Rainbolt raised his pistol, holding his thumb on the hammer.

"No one here has seen them," the trapper said lazily. His eyes moved across the buildings. He looked at something Rainbolt could not see and his gaze was slow and cold. He was a big man there in the yard, with a cruelly tight mouth and jaw and a thin nose. With the sunlight on his dark face his eyes had a pale look. Watching him, Rainbolt wondered how he had thought there was music and warmth in his voice.

"You work for Señor Hudson?" Gondora asked, and there was insulting doubt in his tone.

"In this I am working for him, yes."

"With no horse?"

"A man may go far on foot, Gondora."

"It is true, even into the ground."

The trapper's smile was no more than a quirk of his tight lips. He kept watching the house.

Arriving so soon on Rainbolt's heels, the trapper must be one of the men who had chased Shaun and Rainbolt across the pass. If he was, the chances were that Shaun was dead. In cold fury Rainbolt sighted on the man's chest.

If he knew for sure that the man in the yard was one of the pursuers, he would walk out and kill him. Doubt ticked slowly against Rainbolt's anger. He did not know the man. He could be, indeed, someone working for Hudson; and there was no doubt that residents of the Huerfano took Hudson's cattle when they pleased. Then, too, this man would be a fool to come alone to the Huerfano if he was after the gold.

Gondora was saying, "I have seen no cows with calves. My sons have not seen them. My nephews have not seen them. There is nothing here for you. It would be well for you to look somewhere else for that which you seek."

The faint smile touched the trapper's lips again. He said, "Thanks for the suggestion, old one," and walked away. From the window Rainbolt watched him going unhurriedly down the valley.

Rainbolt went outside into the quadrangle. A half dozen men were lounging there, brown men with knives and pistols in their belts. One of them said, "We should have killed him, Dimasio."

Gondora growled his answer. "We do not kill white fur trappers here, no matter how evil their hearts. I have said this before. Now go up the trail to see what has become of our friend Shaun Weymouth."

The men went toward the corrals. Across the yard the woman called Paisano watched Rainbolt for a moment before she bent again to her work at a *metate*. Gondora strode toward Rainbolt.

"The man knew you," Rainbolt said.

"He has been here before. Last year he tried to steal Paisano and take her to the mountains with him." Gondora shrugged. "He has no love for us here. Perhaps my son was right and we should have killed him; but many trappers spend winters here and it would not be good for us if we killed one of them, even the most evil one."

"You know his name?"

Gondora butchered the word but it came out "McCracken."

Fury ripped through Rainbolt. He strode out into the yard. McCracken had already turned around a small hill thrusting into the valley and was out of sight.

"Do not worry," Gondora said. "He knows beyond doubt that you are here, although we covered for a long distance the tracks of your horse. What is there that he can do now?"

"By God, he killed Shaun!"

Gondora shook his head. "That is beyond belief. Only a great number of Indians will ever kill Shaun, one day when he has grown old like me, but that is a long time away."

Rainbolt kept walking.

"No! Do not be a fool. Come here and listen to what I will say."

There was a power of authority in Gondora's voice. He was Shaun's friend and he seemed to know what he was doing. Rainbolt went back to him. For the first time he noticed knots of curious people on the other side of the river and groups that had come down the trail from the upper part of the valley to see what was going on at Dimasio Gondora's house.

Rainbolt and Gondora went inside the room where the panniers were. "He will not go far," Gondora said. "It was the gold that brought him here. He will be somewhere close if you wish later to kill him." He cocked a shrewd eye toward the panniers. "The gold made a strange noise when you lifted it from the horse."

"What do you mean?"

"It spoke more like stones from a mine than soft gold from a river."

"Who said we got it from a river?"

"No one has said anything. It is only a matter to wonder about."

"Don't get too curious," Rainbolt said.

He saw anger in Gondora's eyes, but the man held on to his politeness. He turned away and went out.

Rainbolt gave the panniers a kick. Damn it, where was Shaun?

Roman Aragon beat his nephew Chico for a time, and then it occurred to him to ask for details about the loss of the burro. It was hot in the sun, so Aragon took the boy inside. He would lie of course; he would tell a thousand lies. It was a curse to have to support a worthless nephew who could not do a man's work and who was always losing valuable property.

Aragon sat down. "Now, the truth."

"I am hungry."

"Your belly is a curse!" Aragon slapped Chico back against the wall. "Now stand there and tell me the truth."

"There were Indians. They came while I was searching over the camping place of the Spanish governor —"

"There! What were you doing so far from Rito Oso where you were sent?"

"I was going later along the mountains to see —"

"You lie!" Aragon slapped the boy again.

"I do not lie. I saw the Utes. They tried to catch the burro in the trees but it ran away from them and went where they could not ride. I followed its tracks. It went toward the San Luis."

"Back to Costilla," Aragon said savagely. It was a long trip, but perhaps on the way back he could find a few more of the crazy gringo's cows to pay him for his trouble.

"It was then while I was hiding in the rocks that the big one called Shaun and the one who brought me here upon his horse came riding up the pass in a great hurry. Shaun went back and shot his rifle and then he ran after the horses."

"More of your Indians, I suppose?"

"No. There were more white men chasing

the first two. They came riding fast on the big red horses from Señor Hudson's house and later there was more shooting, but this I did not see."

Aragon forgot to slap his nephew. Trappers chasing each other? There had been a great weight of some kind in the panniers of the calico that the ugly one with the dried blood on his face had led here a few minutes before. Things of value were often small and heavy. The Fathers of long ago had spoken of gold in the San Juan, and that was where Shaun Weymouth went every winter.

"You rode upon the spotted horse with the panniers," Aragon said. "What was in them?"

"I do not know. The man lifted me up and my feet did not touch the panniers where the weight was."

"Ah! Let us hear more."

"Of the burro I could not catch?" Chico asked.

"No, you little fool! Of the trappers who fought each other."

"That is all. The first two came, chased by the others. There were four. They went up the pass and I came home. In the morning the one who brought me here came upon me as I was resting beside the trail."

"Sleeping, after losing my burro," Aragon

said, but his mind was on other business. Even now in Dimasio Gondora's house there must be a great amount of gold.

"You saw no more than the men chasing each other?"

"That is all. I was too frightened to call to Shaun. They ran back down the mountain to shoot, and then they returned and took the horses up the trail quickly, with the panniers jumping and bouncing out from the side of the spotted horse as if they were empty."

"Empty? There was weight in them when he was here."

"That is true. I felt it when I got down from the spotted horse. I felt the weight of stones in the panniers."

"Stones? You do not imagine this? It is not another of your lies, boy?"

"There were stones in the panniers," Chico said stoutly. "I heard them bump together once when the spotted horse jumped over a log as I was riding him."

Stones when the packhorse came to the Huerfano, and nothing when it had been upon the pass? And yet two trappers had been running from four. Gringo trappers were strange, fierce people, but they did not fight among themselves because of nothing. If there was no gold now in Gondora's house, nothing but stones, there must have been gold in the panniers at some time or the four would not have chased the two.

Aragon thought about it. There was a mystery here. A smart man often could get rich from a mystery. He did not notice when Chico crept away to get something to eat. Aragon went out in the shade where wine hung cool under the trees in a goatskin bag. He refreshed himself and observed how curious people were wandering down the valley toward Gondora's house.

Roman Aragon had done well from stealing horses, and this fall he had planned to take the cattle he had hidden in a little valley near the Arkansas to the pueblo at the mouth of the Fountain where he could sell them. All this was nothing now. He drank more wine. Gold. He would say nothing. He would listen much. Gold could take him from this valley, to Santa Fe, even to Mexico City, where he would be a great man because of his wealth.

But where was the gold?

He called to Chico. He would question the boy more. But Chico had disappeared. Aragon drank from the goatskin bag and thought of Mexico City.

He saw the pale-eyed one go by, the one Gondora's sons and nephews had wanted to kill last year after the trouble over Paisano. McCracken, yes, that was his name. The way he walked, carelessly, yet with springy grace, seeing everything about him, reminded Aragon of one of the great cats of the mountains. There was raw, wild power in all these gringo trappers. They were violent, dangerous men. Aragon himself was no stranger to the mountains but he knew he was not like these gringo trappers. He stood in awe of them, and so he hated them.

He watched McCracken pass. It was very likely that McCracken was one of those who had pursued the spotted packhorse. It would be well to observe what happened when McCracken went to Dimasio Gondora's house; for that, of a certainty, was where he was going. It was no great distance, but Aragon got his horse. As he rode down the river he saw other people moving in the same direction. There were many sharp eyes on the Huerfano.

Aragon tied his horse at the corner of Pablo Puez's maize field and went the rest of the way on foot. He joined Luis Mendoza and Scipio Espinoza, who with others were standing a respectful distance from Gondora's house, listening to what was going on.

At first Aragon felt the catch of fear. The pale-eyed one was speaking of stolen cows.

He said he worked for Señor Hudson. This could be, but last week when Aramante Luna had stopped at Señor Hudson's on his way from Taos, he had reported that the lazy Escobars and their cousins from Costilla were still the only ones working for Señor Hudson.

Scipio gave Aragon a sly look. There were many who knew of the stolen cows and who was hiding them. Gondora knew also; he was an old devil who knew everything that went on in this valley.

But no one here, not even Gondora, was going to speak of cows to a gringo trapper. A few cows of no great value, which would have been killed by wolves anyway if Aragon had not brought them from the mountains and given them a good place to eat grass and men to watch over them day and night.

"The gringo is not interested in cows," Scipio murmured. "He is interested in the other trapper who is hidden in Gondora's house."

That was so, Aragon decided. Of course it was so. He watched the way the pale-eyed one studied the house and looked at Gondora's sons and nephews. He was fearless, this McCracken, but he would be killed quickly if he tried to enter Dimasio Gondora's house without permission. This was what the crowd had come to see.

Gondora was polite and he was like iron. The trapper found out nothing except what he could guess. He went on down the valley and the crowd was disappointed because nothing had happened.

Aragon asked Luis Mendoza, "What did he seek, if it was not cows?"

"Ask your nephew. There has been a great chase across the mountains. Many Indians and trappers are dead. Shaun Weymouth, who used to come here, is dead. The one in Gondora's house came into this valley with something very heavy in the panniers of his horse. What is carried in sacks and is very heavy, Aragon?"

"I do not know," Aragon said. That worthless Chico, that loser of burros, was telling everything. He must be found and beaten into silence quickly.

"Gold of course," Scipio said. "Even now there is a fortune in gold in Gondora's house, guarded by the trapper. It is said that gringo soldiers from the fort in the San Luis will soon be here to protect it and carry it away."

Pablo Puez said, "From my house I saw the trapper lift the panniers from the spotted horse. He would have no help. He lifted them alone and he staggered with their great weight. He is a young, strong man and he staggered."

"You are all fools," Aragon said. "You have been listening to old women talking." He went away to find Chico. That was not difficult, for Chico was with Gondora's grandsons, sitting on the rails of a corral behind Gondora's house. "Come with me, you loser of burros."

Aragon was in a black rage by the time he reached home. He knocked Chico down in the yard and kicked him inside. "You have told every big ear on the Huerfano about the empty panniers you saw!"

"No! I said nothing of that. I told only of the Indians and trappers who chased each other."

"Nothing of the empty panniers?" After a time Aragon was sure that his nephew was telling the truth. "If you speak one word of the panniers, I will hang you by your feet in the sun and beat you with a whip. This is understood?"

"Yes, yes!"

"Now, tell me again just where upon the pass you saw the panniers when they were empty."

Chico described the place. Aragon knew it very well. Several years before he had killed a wounded Comanche not far from there. "The pursuers were close upon the others?"

"Very close."

Aragon went back to the wine bag to think. If the pale-eyed one and his men, who were undoubtedly all dead now, along with Shaun Weymouth, had been close to the packhorse on the pass, there would not have been much time for them to hide the gold; yet Shaun and his friend had got rid of it in some manner, perhaps tossing it into the bushes or dropping it into a deep beaver pond.

The pursuers had stolen Señor Hudson's tall red horses and had used them in the chase. The spotted horse that had come here was a scrubby Ute pony. If it had carried a great weight of gold far, it would have been tired on the pass, so tired that the red horses would have caught up with it, which indeed they almost had when it was carrying nothing but empty panniers. It must be, therefore, knowing that they were being chased by men on fresh, strong horses, that Shaun and his friend had got rid of their gold somewhere between the Hudson ranch and the place where Chico had seen them.

There must have been gold. Why else would the trapper now at Gondora's house have made such a great pretense?

McCracken had been deceived; Aragon

was not. He would go back at once across the pass and study every track and mark. No sooner was the thought worked out when he heard a heavy voice singing. For a moment Aragon thought he was seeing an apparition.

Shaun Weymouth was coming. One side of his face was blood-caked and swollen. There was old blood on the left sleeve of his buckskin shirt. He came down the trail in great strides, swinging his rifle, singing a strange song. A dog ran out at him, snarling. Shaun looked at it and roared something in an Indian tongue Aragon did not understand.

The dog fell back. It howled and ran away and Shaun's laughter caused people to come from their houses and stare at him as if he were crazy. He must be drunk, Aragon thought, or else he had killed a dozen men and was singing a victory song.

Chico came from somewhere and started to run after the trapper. Aragon shouted at the boy, who came back reluctantly, sullen and afraid. "Go play with Dimasio Gondora's grandsons," Aragon directed. "Listen to what is said by the trappers. Listen well and tell me everything and if you do well I will not beat you again for a month."

"Yes, Uncle." Chico ran quickly after Shaun.

Chico did not come back until very late. He was tired and sleepy, for he had stuffed himself and stolen wine at Gondora's house, where there had been a feast to honor the arrival of Shaun Weymouth.

"What was said?" Aragon demanded.

"There was a quarrel between the one called Rainbolt and Dimasio's oldest son over the Paisano."

"I am not interested in that!"

"Shaun said an evil spell on him had been broken by his arrival here, and that was why —"

"I have no interest in that!"

"There was no gold in the panniers, but rocks, as I said before. We had stolen wine, Pedro and Juanito and I, and were drinking it in the shadows beside the room where the trappers stay. Inside Shaun made his tremendous laugh and told the one called Rainbolt that he should have told Dimasio there was no gold in the panniers because Dimasio could be trusted with any secret."

"And then?"

"I do not know. Rainbolt talked in English in a low voice, and then Josepha, who knew we had stolen the wine, came with a stick and we ran away across the river."

"What of the men who chased Shaun and his friends?"

"They are all dead but the one who came here."

That might be, Aragon thought; it was convenient to believe, at least. McCracken thought the gold was in Gondora's house. Let him think so. For three days, at least, there would be a celebration there to honor Shaun's arrival.

Aragon had time to work. He was ahead of everyone.

"Tomorrow, Chico, I go to see about my cows near the Arkansas. That is where I will be. It is understood?"

"Yes, Uncle."

Before daylight Aragon rode down the valley. A few dogs barked at him. The houses were dark and quiet, but he knew there were those who heard him pass. After a time he circled and started toward Mosca Pass.

He was on his way to become a rich man.

CHAPTER EIGHT

John Hudson sat in his house after breakfast at the big springs and watched his daughter Gail cleaning up the room. She was deft and positive in all her actions, carrying on her morning routine with a sureness that irritated Hudson. Women were that way: They had certain unimportant daily tasks to perform and they learned them by habit, doing their work with their mind on something else. They never had to face the sudden jarring complexities of a man's life.

Gail had stayed after Alice left, neither offering her father comforting words after the betrayal nor condemning her mother. She had shut herself away from her father. She had insulted him and yet he never could bring the issue to a quarrel, no matter how he tried. It had been that way with Alice too, the last five years of their married life.

Hudson ran his hand across his dark, wavy hair. The edges of it were gray. When he shaved or when he trimmed his sideburns, he always saw a handsome face staring back at him from the mirror, a face with clear gray eyes and strong features. It puzzled him, for the face was always so confident and determined with never a trace of the inner man that had been tormenting him ever since he came to this forlorn country.

"About those five men who came here yesterday, Gail —" Hudson said, and waited for his daughter to make some comment that would ease his way to the explanation in his mind.

"What about them?"

"There were five of them. You saw the kind of men they were, barbarians straight out of the mountains. I don't see how anyone could have kept them from taking the stock."

"I suppose not," Gail said.

"You suppose? You're always casting doubt on my personal courage. How could I have stopped them?"

Gail was sweeping ashes from the hearth back into the fireplace. Later in the day the wind would start once more and then the ashes would be blown in a feathery fan across the floor again. The broom was spruce boughs tied to a stick. Diaz Escobar had made it for her. She put the broom in the angle of the fireplace stones and logs and stood regarding it a moment before she turned to face her father.

"There's nothing you could have done," she said. "I saw the men. They wanted the sorrels and the mules to chase the other two."

That was the answer that Hudson had wanted but now it did not suit him. "No doubt you think that gawky savage you made such a fuss over the other night could have saved the stock."

"I made no fuss over him. I was looking at the mountains. He came over and talked to me."

"Yes, I heard. You had to bring your mother into the conversation. Talking about Alice to a half wild trapper." Hudson shook his head.

"I won't quarrel, Father."

"No! You won't quarrel! You'll just stand there and condemn me for a coward. Everything I've done out here has been wrong and I know it, but little consolation I've gotten from the very people who might have given it."

"What do you want me to say?"

"Nothing!" Hudson shouted. He rose and took his rifle from the pegs over the door and walked out. Gail heard him shouting to Diaz and Bernal Escobar, two of his helpers who had returned late last night from hunting. The other three Mexicans undoubtedly were by now visiting in Costilla and would return when they pleased with an involved story of having pursued a wounded elk until they were lost, or having been chased by Utes for three days.

Gail stood by the door, looking at the mountains. Five years ago her father had been an idol, everything that a father and a wealthy Virginia planter ought to be. And then she had begun to see the flaws in him, the way he had to work himself into a rage before he fought a duel, his alternate spells of arrogance and deep humility before his wife.

Two years ago, seeking something that was lacking inside him, John Hudson had made the fatal mistake of exposing his character to a wild, raw land.

Five strong men had taken his stock. Hudson could have died trying to prevent it, and that was all he could have done; and yet, although he shouted that fact, he could not accept it. Now he had built up anger enough to go after the horses, but unless Bernal and Diaz accomplished the task, Hudson would fail again.

This was a land of sharp emergencies. John Hudson had not been born with the qualities to meet them, and his daughter knew that fact too well.

She saw her father ride away with the Escobars, two short men with Indian features. They were tough-looking men, the best of the five Hudson employees, but they were only as tough as their leader. Gail Hudson hoped that they would never come close to finding the stock, for it would mean only another frustration for her father, another vial of acid inside him, another personal defeat.

Gail looked out through the cottonwoods on the immense valley fading into the distance, narrowing as it lifted northward where ranges of blue mountains waited far beyond the end of the Blood of Christ range.

Because of what John Hudson had been before they knew him well, one of them had been obliged to stay here, Gail or her mother. Hudson would never know that they had cut a deck of cards to see who won and who lost. Gail had won. She could have left, but because she had two parents whom she loved, she had forced her mother to go.

Time and distance were the killers in this land. Gail looked on both and turned away to the small tasks that helped a woman forget.

That tall young trapper who had been here over night . . . How far away was he now, how much closer to realizing any dreams he had? The gentleness and the obvious woman hunger in him as he had talked to her in the yard had upset and excited her, so that during much of the night she had been awake and had heard the quiet padding around outside.

When the two men left very early in the morning she had been wide awake, standing with the thin-scraped deer hide of her bedroom window pulled back slightly from the frame.

Passing the house the young trapper had murmured, "That Hudson's daughter is a woman I'd like to have, Shaun."

The old man was surly. "You don't expect to get that kind for hawk bells, do you?"

Afterward Gail sat down on her bed, strangely yearning and tense, thinking about hawk bells. Trinkets traded to Indian women for favors. She was in nowise insulted.

She was a lonely woman in a wild country, and she was young, but her thinking about Rainbolt came from more than that. She had known few young men that she respected fully. Rainbolt was of a different breed, quiet, courteous from more than manners, a tough, virile man who would have stood out in any society. She would have been attracted to him wherever she met him, but she had carefully hidden her interest when he was here.

Hawk bells . . . Gail Hudson had never

collected them but she knew they came in many forms.

Hudson and the Escobars were out of sight when Gail looked from the doorway again. She gazed across the valley toward the La Garitas, down the line of travel on which she had first seen the young trapper coming toward the house.

She didn't even know his name, but she knew a man when she saw one, and he had been that. By now he would be well on his way down the Arkansas, she supposed. Gail Hudson went back to work. She had to keep her hands busy, her mind occupied with everyday tasks, or there would come a day when she would begin to destroy herself like her father.

Perhaps next week Lieutenant Merriam would arrange to bring a scouting patrol from the fort this way again. He was young. He stood in awe of her for some reason. His desire to be transferred from duty at the fort ran through all his conversation, but he was in love with Gail . . . and that was something.

John Hudson rode at the head of his command, the two Escobars, with a slight frown on his brow. He looked like an able leader who knew exactly what he was about. When the Escobars began to range about on both sides of the trail, like hunting dogs, he was disturbed. He preferred compactness, but he did not bother to call his helpers in.

They struck the foot of the pass beyond the sand dunes. Hudson saw the marks of shod horses in the earth and gave them brief attention. The tough little pony he was riding was the one the Escobars had used as a packhorse to bring in a deer last night. Its sides were stained with deer blood and the flies kept following it. Hudson felt demeaned by having to ride it. His rage against the men who had taken his stock burned steadily. When he was angry he could act. It was only when he was caught suddenly with no chance to prepare himself mentally that he became confused and uncertain.

Diaz said excitedly, "Señor Hudson, the tracks!"

"Of course. I saw them."

Diaz looked at Bernal. "But they go the wrong way! The fresh ones are of the mules and horses coming this way!"

Hudson stared down at the trail. He saw all by itself a fresh print and it was pointed toward the valley instead of up the pass. "I'm not sure those are my stock."

"But they are!" Diaz got down and began to point out peculiarities of the marks.

"I believe you're right," Hudson said.

"They went up and came down, at least some of them."

"All of them," Bernal said.

Hudson stared back at the dunes. He was confused.

"They have ridden into the sand, which covers tracks quickly," Diaz said. "Beyond the dunes we will find the tracks again."

Hudson nodded thoughtfully. "I believe you're right."

On the valley side of the dunes the Escobars picked up the tracks again, where they emerged from the sand and turned northward.

"There is only one man, Señor," Diaz reported. "He is leading three animals. He is going toward Antelope Springs."

"Then he will soon be a dead man," Hudson said grimly.

Green River had his troubles. He had stopped to rest the horses and mules and catch a little sleep at one of the big seeps at Antelope Springs. From the cottonwoods he saw the soldiers, seven of them, making a little tour down in the direction of San Luis Creek, and then they disappeared into the swales and he had seen no more of them.

He lay at the edge of the trees, searching the country and worrying, wondering if the cavalrymen had spotted his dust when he was headed toward the grove. They just might be playing it cute, lying low in the swales, waiting for him to show himself. He had no love for troopers, and officers were always damned curious, and here he was with four stolen animals that every person in the valley undoubtedly would recognize on sight.

The best thing was to wait it out until night. A fine peck of trouble McCracken had got him into this time; but Green River had been in worse fixes. He settled down to his waiting, dozing at intervals, rousing to scan the country.

If John Hudson had not shouted something at the wrong time, he and the two Mexicans would have caught Green River completely by surprise. They had come quietly into the grove on foot while Green River's attention was on the place where he had last seen the cavalrymen. But Hudson saw the sorrels and called out, "There they are!"

Green River came lunging up from behind a log with his pistol cocked. He saw three men, and the best he could hope for was to get out of it with his life, forgetting the animals picketed near the seep.

The Escobars waited for Hudson to make

the first move. His rifle was in his hand, and although he was covered, the odds were on the side with the most men.

It was another emergency that trapped Hudson with its suddenness. A man had a pistol on him. If he made any rash moves, he would be shot. The Escobars were somewhere close behind him, but he decided that they would be as shocked as he was. Beyond that, it had come about too fast for him to figure a way out.

Green River saw the indecision in the man and gave Hudson no chance to recover and think. A glance told him that the Mexicans were not going to make any play until their boss set the temper of things. Green River said, "Drop that rifle!"

Hudson's face turned red. He tried to raise anger that would drive him into action. Given time, he might have succeeded, but the immediate threat of the pistol left him no time.

He dropped the rifle. The Escobars, taking their cue from him, disarmed themselves at Green River's command; and then Green River, playing it to the hilt, marched them from the grove.

They got on their horses and rode away. Green River heard Hudson curse his men savagely. Somehow there seemed to be a trick in all of it, and soldiers or no soldiers, Green River decided it was time to make his run.

He got the sorrels and the mules and headed north. A half hour later he ran straight into the seven cavalrymen who had just risen from a long nooning in the dry grass of a swale.

Lieutenant Merriam said, "By God, those are Hudson's sorrels!"

Green River did not even bother to tell any lies. His eyes slid over the soldiers and he kept telling himself that they were not the civil law. They let Green River go. A sergeant protested that returning stolen animals to civilians was not Army business, and Merriam shut him up in a hurry.

They left Green River on foot and rode away with the mules and sorrels. Lieutenant Merriam said, "It's high time we scouted the foot of Mosca Pass anyway, Sergeant."

The sergeant kept a straight face and said, "Yes, sir."

CHAPTER NINE

Next to Indians and soldiers, Green River hated walking. After the scouting detail left, he sat down and figured out his position. The soldiers had thrown his personal gear on the ground and left him his weapons. That was all to the good, but he still had to have a horse.

Somewhere on the pass were the two ponies that he had abandoned in favor of a mule after Shaun killed Ben Onstead, the first casualty of the original five. Perhaps by now they had wandered down to where the grass was good near the mouth of Medano Creek. If he could not find them, he would go back by night to the Hudson ranch and steal the sorrels.

He gathered up his gear and began to walk. When he went through the grove he observed that the soldiers had picked up the weapons that he had made Hudson and his Mexicans throw down.

He cursed every inch of the twelve-mile walk back to Medano Creek. He crossed the jumble of tracks where Hudson had turned back from going up the pass.

When he came to where Shaun and Rainbolt had crossed soft ground, he rested for a time, studying the tracks from habit. The way the packhorse had sunk into the earth, it must have been carrying two hundred pounds of gold. That scrubby little calico must have been all iron and rawhide to hold out on the pass against fresh horses.

Suddenly Green River's eyes grew tight and narrow, and all his instincts for reading sign sharpened. There was no doubt that the hoofs of the packhorse had sunk in deeply. Before, in their haste to get on with the chase, he and the others had ridden wide of this particular spot in order to preserve sign and make a brief study of it. Green River saw now that they had been in too much haste.

Both Shaun and Rainbolt had ridden close to the packhorse before they went out into the soft ground. They must have swung over on its back, both of them. Green River took his time, and at last he was satisfied. The gold had never gone up the pass.

The nerves in Green River's face began to tingle. He looked all around him carefully. The ranch? No. Hudson was not the kind of man Shaun would trust for a minute. Somewhere between here and the ranch? Unlikely because it was all poor country to make a cache without leaving all kinds of sign.

Green River stared at the great dunes. A sly, knowing smile bunched the scar tissue on the ruined side of his face. He was still in the game. Those soldiers had done him a big favor.

Deliberately he walked back and forth in the soft ground until he had made all sign unreadable, and then he went on up the trail to search for the ponies and a place to camp so that he could watch the dunes.

A few miles up the trail, going very slowly, was Roman Aragon. He had seen two dead men, one at the falls on the other side of the pass, the second with his face pressed out of shape against the rocks on top of the pass. The sight had not bothered him in the least; it was proof that much had been at stake.

At times he dismounted and walked out from the trail, peering into the bushes, exploring the rocks. When he passed beaver ponds close to the trail, he was very careful. Sometimes he probed into them with a long pole.

From a turn above the timber he saw the dunes. Was the gold down there in the sand that hid all marks of things that touched it?

Yes, it very well might be so; that was what Aragon would have done. But he was in no hurry. He would come to the dunes in time, if he did not find what he was after before then.

In a narrow place in the trail he found a third dead man. The growing proof of how Shaun had fought with cold ferocity gave Aragon pause. Aragon stared uneasily at the dead man. Now he knew that in all there had been five men after Shaun and his friend. The fifth one had run away at the falls, taking the horses and the mules. With a haul like that he would not stop for a long time.

There were dangers in this hunting gold. There must be, also, a great amount of wealth. Aragon went around the dead man and on down the trail.

He found sign that he did not like. A man wearing moccasins had come up the pass some time this afternoon. He had come this far and then he had turned off into the aspen thickets. Aragon followed the tracks. The man was trailing two unshod horses. A Ute? It must be, although many men wore moccasins. Let the man find his horses and go on his way. Roman Aragon would not bother him unless he was an Indian and came near enough to be killed.

At sunset Aragon was close to the dunes. He mounted his horse and sat looking down on them. Many mysteries that no man would ever see lay beneath those huge brown ridges. And now it seemed most likely that there was gold beneath the sand somewhere. Aragon rode on down to the dunes. He came to a place where the man with moccasins had made much sign in damp earth. It was very puzzling.

Riding softly on the skirts of the dunes, Aragon considered the huge task before him. It would be foolish to go probing blindly into the sand. He went into the junipers on the hills to the south of the sand and camped. Until dark gently obscured the hollows and the black-maned ridges, he sat staring at the dunes.

Like a prowling wolf Frank McCracken roamed the hills beyond Gondora's house on the Huerfano. In two days he learned much about the movements of the household. Ten grown men, at least, lived with Gondora; a bold strike against the place was out of the question. It was far better to wait until Shaun and Rainbolt started away alone, which should be soon. Rainbolt was young. He would never have the patience to live under miserable conditions when he had gold.

McCracken kept for the most part on the down-river side of the Gondora house. When Shaun and Rainbolt left, they would of course go east. On the third day of his vigil McCracken went down the trail two miles and set a trap. He was desperately hungry, afraid to steal from the houses at night for fear his presence would be discovered and warn Shaun and Rainbolt; afraid to go back into the hills to kill deer, lest Shaun and Rainbolt leave while he was gone.

McCracken's luck was good. The first man up the trail that morning was a Mexican trader towing a well-laden mule. McCracken stumbled out in front of the man, staggering, holding his chest with one hand. When he was close enough to know that the lead mule could not escape, he shot the trader as the man was dismounting to help him.

McCracken covered his tracks well. He dumped the trader's body in a gully for the crows and ravens to pick. He picketed the two mules in a small aspen park. Now he had food and he had animals to carry out his plans. He settled to the watch once more.

He came to know the movement of every young shepherd who left Gondora's house in the morning, the leisurely actions of the women about the place, and the irritating inactivity of Shaun and Rainbolt. They were in no hurry to leave, at least Shaun, who sat in the sun in the early morning and slept in the shade in the hot afternoons.

Rainbolt was much with Paisano. He seemed to tag her about her chores in the daytime, and in the early evening McCracken saw them walking together near the river. Except for the gold, McCracken would have been waiting with a ready knife some evening when Rainbolt strolled with the woman in the trees by the Huerfano. She was something, that young Indian wench. McCracken remembered how she had struggled against him when he had tried to carry her off last year, strong and supple and yet full of woman softness.

After a week on the Huerfano, Jim Rainbolt had lost patience. He had made a new stock for his rifle. He had bought with the small pouch of gold in his plunder sack a mule and two horses from one of Gondora's sons. And during the evenings he had made love to Paisano; but even that did not compensate for the worry he felt over unprotected gold in the sand dunes.

This afternoon he went to the cottonwoods and woke Shaun rudely from his accustomed nap. "We've stalled long enough, Shaun. Let's get back over the hill and pick it up."

Shaun opened one eye. "That gold won't spoil, boy."

"You've been acting funny lately, Shaun."

"Just resting. I like it here."

"I don't." Rainbolt cast a disgusted look around the place. Paisano and an old woman were butchering a goat. Everyone else was asleep. About dusk things would liven up. Shaun would be in his glory, telling tall tales, dancing with the women like he was a youngster. There would be more peppery food, more singing, more boasting, great stories of what Shaun and Gondora had done in the old days in Apache country to the south.

And Rainbolt would catch only about half of the fast-flowing Spanish. He had grasped even less at times when he was sure that Gondora and Shaun were discussing him.

"Let's go get the stuff, I say." Rainbolt was angry.

"Sure we will." Shaun grinned. "You coming back for Paisano afterwards?"

"I'm going east."

"Yeah." Shaun's face grew quiet. "Wouldn't do to take her there, huh?"

"Who said I was going to take her anywhere?"

"She's your woman, boy."

Rainbolt moved restlessly. "When are we going back over the hill?"

"There ain't no hurry. Maybe Green River did run out, like Gondora's boys say, but

133

McCracken didn't. You saw him here and now he's waiting for us somewhere."

"All right, so he is! There were five before."

"I know," Shaun said bleakly. "You're in such a damned killing hurry." He rolled over and looked at the sky through the trees.

"You act like you don't want to go back, Shaun."

The old man was silent.

"You didn't lie to me — about the number of steps, or anything else?"

A darkness showed in Shaun's eyes. "That's enough of that," he warned quietly.

"Then what are you stalling about?"

"Easy, boy. Don't get rough with me."

"I'm going," Rainbolt said. "Tomorrow."

Shaun studied the younger man for a long time. "I've always heard that gold raised hell with friendship."

"It hasn't changed anything, except that I'm not waiting any longer. Don't you want the gold?"

Shaun frowned. He looked up through the trees again. "I worked for it. I ran with it. I killed men over it. Sure, I guess I want it as bad as you do."

"Then let's go get it."

"What are you going to do about Paisano?"

"That's my business."

"Sure it is," Shaun said. "You know what I'd do, was I your age? I'd take her and head right back for the mountains. I did that my first time out. It's been a long time ago. I think I'd do it all over again."

"When do we start? I've got the horses for you and me and a mule for the gold."

Shaun's thoughts came back from a long way off. "Why, tonight is as good a time as any, I suppose."

"We'll be there by daylight."

"No, we won't. We'll go down to the Arkansas and up the river and across the range —"

"What for!"

"You can trust Gondora," Shaun said, "but around a place like this facts leak out like water seeping through a bullberry bush. I misdoubt there's anyone here that don't know you hauled rocks in them panniers."

"That's all the more reason we ought to be on our way."

"Nobody but us is going to get that gold, boy. Maybe we didn't fool anybody here, but I'm pretty damned sure we tolled in McCracken. Even if he's caught on, or gotten suspicious, he'd wait around to trail us back. Now, we wouldn't want to make things too easy, too clear for him, would we, boy? That's why we're going up the Arkansas with loaded panniers."

"McCracken's gone back across the hill."

"No, he ain't. Gondora tells me that a trader who should have been here a couple, three days back has plumb disappeared. He had two mules when he left the Fountain."

"That's another of your hunches, Shaun."

"Nope. These Mexicans know what's going on for a hundred miles around them, maybe farther. I'll bet you my medicine pouch McCracken got them mules, and I'll bet you he's within two long rifle shots of here. When I had time, I was going looking for him, but we can toll him out anyway. He'll be on our trail tomorrow."

Shaun rolled on his side, pillowed his head on his arms and went to sleep.

Rainbolt stared at him a moment and then went to the corrals to look at the horses.

Paisano said, "You are leaving?"

"You hear too much."

"I heard nothing. I see it on your face." Paisano gave Rainbolt a long, direct look. She asked no questions.

She turned her eyes to her work, using the knife with deft, strong strokes. She was the most fiery and the most gentle Indian woman Rainbolt had ever known. He could feel her mood now, one of strong condemnation, but there was no humility, no begging, in her.

"I'll be back, Paisano."

She did not answer. Rainbolt went on toward the corrals a few steps. He turned and went back to the woman. "I said I would be back."

She gave him a quiet, bitter look. She called him a liar without saying anything, and bent once more to cutting up the goat. The old woman beside her spat, looking at Rainbolt from wise, hating eyes. She glanced at the knife in her hand and drew it with a deliberate gesture across a piece of meat.

That was the trouble with getting mixed up with women anywhere, Rainbolt thought. Even in Indian camps it was not as simple as some people thought to walk away from a squaw any old time you wished to leave. There were all kinds of complications: relatives, gifts, arguments beyond end. If he had found Paisano in an Indian camp, perhaps he might have been like Shaun, who had loved the same Blackfoot woman for ten years, until the Crows killed her in a raid.

Rainbolt had not found it as easy as Paisano thought to turn away from her just now. If it were not for the gold . . . but that was the important thing just now. To buy these three animals, he had given Gondora's son, José, almost all his gold. Once it would have meant nothing to be without money of any kind, but Rainbolt was a rich man now.

That complicated his problem with Paisano. Because he was wealthy, it seemed logical that he should go back home, but Paisano would not like it there. Even in St. Louis, where there were many women of Spanish, Indian and Mexican blood, she would not be happy.

Rainbolt tried to test his own thinking for dishonesty. Was it that he was ashamed to take Paisano back home with him? She would go. She would go anywhere with him. He was ashamed of himself, not of Paisano. It must be the gold that had changed his way of thinking.

When he returned from the dunes, he would settle the problem. At the moment, the gold had to come first.

The stars were soft when Shaun and Rainbolt stood ready to leave late that night. Gondora said, "Go with God, and be careful of who follows." It occurred to him to tell certain facts about the activities of Roman Aragon during the last week, but Aragon was of the community, and Gondora had not become the patriarch of the Huerfano by telling the secrets of his own people. He kept his silence.

Rainbolt looked at the shadowy buildings, at the dark backs of animals in the corrals where one of Gondora's sons lay quietly on guard against a raid by Utes. Rainbolt heard the gurgle of the river. He saw the faint outlines of the maize fields. Somewhere up the valley a dog barked sleepily, without enough interest to evoke answers from other dogs.

Shaun was already mounted. "Let's go," he grumbled, surly because of the hour.

Rainbolt kept looking into shadows. She was here somewhere; he felt her presence. He walked toward the dark cottonwoods where Shaun had spent so much time napping. Paisano was there. She thrust a bundle into Rainbolt's hands and he knew what it was, food to be eaten in the saddle.

"I go now," Rainbolt said.

"I have known."

He took Paisano into his arms and for a long moment he wondered why he was so anxious to leave. Shaun was a dim bulk on his horse, saying nothing, but his waiting was like a rebuke. *You're the one that was in such a hurry, Rainbolt.*

"I will come back, Paisano," Rainbolt said.

The woman pushed him away from her, suddenly stiff and resentful. Rainbolt went back to the animals and rode away with Shaun. He asked himself if he had lied about returning. Paisano thought so, surely. Rainbolt did not know; it was a compulsion and an obligation to say that he would come back, but he did not know whether he had spoken truth or not.

CHAPTER TEN

With the afternoon sun in their faces they rode over the long brown hills that bordered the Arkansas. Snowfields lay in the broad flutes of the Blood of Christ Mountains on their left. Beyond the serrated crests were the dunes, but Shaun and Rainbolt were going farther from them with every step.

Shaun had been silent all day. Several times he had dropped back to lie under a hill and watch the back trail. Each time, after he caught up with Rainbolt, he shook his head when Rainbolt asked him what he'd seen.

It was likely, Rainbolt conceded, that McCracken was following them; and he wasn't sure that some of Shaun's Mexican friends were not also back there some place.

They rode until after dusk. They were still not on the Arkansas because Shaun had stayed in the foothills where the going was continually up and down and around steeply cut gulches. At dusk Shaun was doubly alert. They camped on a small stream with high cliffs at their backs and a tiny grassy meadow before them. Although Shaun did not say so, Rainbolt knew that this place had been set in Shaun's mind as the goal for the first day's riding.

Again, as at the Hudson ranch, Shaun was restless in the night, padding along the base of the cliffs, going out to make a circle of the camp, moving quietly among the picketed animals. By dawn his unease had made Rainbolt surly.

"If you're convinced he's back there somewhere, let's hole in and bait a trap for him."

"McCracken can outwait the devil himself." Shaun shook his head. "We won't see him until we hit the valley again."

"You act like you think he's a spirit."

"Make no mistake about it. I got out of one deal when my medicine said I was done. Now I'd like to go on living for a while. My biggest worry is he'll outguess us and be waiting somewhere ahead. He knows by now where we're going."

That was likely, Rainbolt thought; if they really had the gold, they wouldn't be dawdling along in the foothills. They would be out on open ground streaking for the States. "Then why'd we come this way at all, if we ain't fooling no one?"

"I thought he might show up the first day," Shaun said. "By now he's really suspecting we ain't got the gold. No telling what he'll do."

"Sometimes I wish we'd never buried the stuff," Rainbolt said irritably. "We could have gone on foot over the pass, shifting the panniers from horse to horse. We might have made it."

"Hindsight," Shaun said. He went out to watch the back trail. When he returned he said, "I'll go you better than that. Sometimes I wish we'd never found the damned gold in the first place."

"I know," Rainbolt said darkly.

They crossed the Arkansas in mid-morning; but instead of following it, Shaun led the way into the hills on the north side of it, red, piñon-scrabbled hills that ran toward the great Bayou Salade. They came down over rocks in a twisting canyon and forded the river again near the beginning of a gorge, and then Shaun struck southwest up sandy gulches, and they were farther now from the Blood of Christ Mountains than when they had started.

That night they camped in the timber at a spring. Rather than bear the gnawing unease of Shaun's restlessness, Rainbolt persuaded him to break the night into two-hour watches.

Sitting with his rifle across his legs, Rainbolt watched the stars and listened to the night, and wondered bitterly about this constant vigilance against something unseen, the sharp guarding of something unpossessed. Was all this real caution on Shaun's part, or was he stalling, laughing to himself, waiting for the dunes to change and confuse Rainbolt when he tried to recover the gold?

The cold night air bore the creeping rot of suspicion.

At breakfast Rainbolt said, "I don't favor this running in circles, Shaun."

Shaun gave Rainbolt steady scrutiny from sleep-pouched eyes. He turned away and said, "It does look like we're having a heap of trouble over stinking yellow metal that grows wild in the mountains."

His meaning was not quite clear to Rainbolt. "Let's go straight over the mountains from here."

Shaun shook his head.

"What are you stalling about?"

Rainbolt's tone of voice brought a dangerous quiet to Shaun's face, but he turned away again. "There ain't no good pass I know of for a while."

"We'll find one!"

"I ain't killing off my horse sprawling over rocks and through snowbanks where there ain't no way."

"I'm cutting loose today. I'll find a way across the mountains," Rainbolt said.

"Don't be a fool."

"Why would I be a fool? Is there something about those dunes you didn't tell me? Is there something —"

The muzzle of Shaun's rifle came around on Rainbolt. Shaun's eyes were deep and Indian savage. Rainbolt had seen him that way once before when a Crow had jeered him with the worst insult of all, telling him that he had no parents, no brothers, no family. The years of Shaun's brutal existence, the high disregard for life, hung in his expression for a moment before he lowered the rifle slowly.

"Go on alone if you want to," Shaun said.

"Don't ever put that rifle on me again." No, Rainbolt would not go on by himself. He had distrusted the dunes as a place to cache anything from the first. He was more distrustful of them now. They would go there together, and he would be watching Shaun Weymouth every moment.

They rode all day up winding gulches, around tough thickets of oak brush, cutting across the tops of hills when the gulches bore too strongly toward the mountains. At dusk they tumbled down from the pitching hills and came into a wide place in the valley where the river was running slowly and peacefully.

Shaun, who had not talked since morning, pointed toward the bluish snowfields settling into night. "Up there's your pass."

They had gone long miles over rough country, long miles out of their way, it seemed to Rainbolt. He slept with his weapons close at hand when it was Shaun's turn to stand guard. Rainbolt slept very little.

McCracken had the patience of a hungry buffalo wolf, and he had lived like one while watching Gondora's house. When Shaun and Rainbolt went by in the dead of night, he had been close enough to the trail to catch a brief silhouette of them.

That it took him an hour to get back to the mules and supplies he had taken from the Mexican trader he had killed several days before was of no moment. No man trailing Shaun dared press him too closely; McCracken knew that fact quite well by now.

When he came to the first sign that showed how Shaun was protecting his back trail, McCracken grinned. It might be a long haul, but the first man to stumble into a trap would not be McCracken.

The route Shaun and Rainbolt were taking became more puzzling. Men laden with gold and anxious to get out of the country would not wear their horses down by staying in the broken hills. McCracken began to give intense study to the tracks of the pack mule. After two days he was sure that it was not carrying a great weight.

Perhaps Shaun and Rainbolt had made a fool of him, and now they could very well be trying to lead him in the wrong direction. It was unlikely that they would have left the gold on the Huerfano.

Had the gold ever been on the Huerfano at all?

It could be that he had been led on a wild chase like an excited Sioux running buffalo. The farther he followed the trail the more sure he became that Shaun and Rainbolt did not have the gold with them. It was possible, of course, that it was distributed on all three animals. It was possible, too, that Shaun was playing one of his subtle Indian tricks.

It was the line of travel that made McCracken wonder most of all. They were riding with the range. Like as not, as soon as they were sure no one was following them, they would cross to the other side.

Where could they have cached the contents of the panniers during the chase? Not anywhere from the San Juan because Green River had studied their trail every foot of the way. The calico had been heavily overloaded at the Hudson ranch. That much McCracken had got out of the owner before the man had refused to make a horse trade.

Where then on the pass? McCracken had closed the chase much more quickly than he had expected after leaving the ranch. On the way across the mountains there had been no time for Shaun to make a cache. Except where they had ridden through the sand beside the dunes, Shaun and Rainbolt had left tracks that were —

Except at the dunes!

Patient though he was, McCracken was also a desperate gambler. He considered all the facts he knew and he bolstered them with shrewd guesses.

McCracken decided to play the gamble.

On the second day of his lone pursuit he left the trail he was following and turned straight into the Blood of Christ Mountains. Luck was with him. He found an Indian trail that he had never heard any trapper mention. At that, he almost killed the mules before he got across.

The dunes were a distant smear down in an angle of the mountains. McCracken rode toward them. When he got there it would be time again for patience. . . .

CHAPTER ELEVEN

Ducks exploded from San Luis Creek when Shaun and Rainbolt rode down to water their horses. Some of them went down the valley, where, thirty miles away, the pale brown dunes lay against the distance. Shaun seemed reluctant to look that way; he stared, instead, at the crimson wash of sunset on the *Sangre de Cristo,* Blood of Christ Mountains.

"No hurry," he said.

This continual lack of eagerness to reach the dunes was raking the black suspicion of Rainbolt's mind. He himself had dwelt briefly on the advantages of there being but one man to recover the gold; why wouldn't Shaun hold similar thoughts?

During the night Rainbolt heard him coming softly toward where Rainbolt lay. Rainbolt saw him stop and turn as one of the horses stamped restlessly. Holding back the trigger of his pistol, Rainbolt cocked it silently.

Shaun swung away from camp and went out to the animals. Rainbolt let the hammer of his pistol down and tried to sleep, but he found himself listening for Shaun's every movement, distrusting Shaun, and forgetting that there might be other dangers in the night.

Living in Indian country had developed an alertness in Rainbolt that was like second sense, but it had never left him strained and tense the way he was now.

He got up in the morning tired, but the dunes lay pale and waiting in the early light, only thirty miles away. He was eager to be off.

After hours of dusty traveling, they seemed to be no closer. The mountains expanded and landmarks changed but the dunes lay far away like some mysterious, receding mass. Shaun seemed to lag more as the hours passed, giving constant attention to the back trail, saying nothing, frowning over troubles of his own.

"There's nobody behind us!" Rainbolt said.

"I know. Then he must be ahead of us."

There was no use in arguing with Shaun. He was too much of an Indian in his thinking; but he was not so much Indian that he didn't know the value of gold.

Shaun rode loosely in the saddle, worried, grim. Sometimes he changed the position of his rifle as he scanned the country, shifting it above the horn of his saddle; and sometimes the muzzle swept carelessly across Rainbolt's body.

Rainbolt had periods of cold argument with himself. He had been three years with Shaun Weymouth. They had been partners and they had never questioned faith in each other. But something had changed in Shaun the day they started out of the San Juan with a fortune. Perhaps all winter long the sight of gold had started something corroding inside him. He was a white man, no matter how long he had been out here.

Rainbolt drew his pistol slowly and let it rest on his thigh away from Shaun. Every careless sweep of the big rifle in Shaun's hands made Rainbolt's belly muscles tighten.

The dunes at last came closer. But there were still miles to ride beside them before reaching the southern shoulder. The pistol in Rainbolt's hand grew hot from the sun. His grip upon it was slippery with sweat.

By making affairs as unpleasant as possible for others, John Hudson managed to forget a great deal of his dissatisfaction with himself. The last three of the Escobars — their names were not Escobar but it was convenient to call them that because they were relatives of Diaz and Bernal — had returned from their private jaunt with a remarkable story of having fought off a large party of Utes and Apaches, as far as Hudson could get a translation of their story from Diaz.

Hudson promptly put them to work hoeing potatoes. They were not getting much done, but at least they had to stand in the hot sun and suffer. Hudson had sent Bernal and Diaz out to round up some cattle, more to get rid of the two men than for any practical reasons.

Hudson was sick of the sight of Bernal and Diaz. With silence they had condemned him all the way back from the frustrating attempt to recover the sorrels and the mules.

From his chair in the shade, with a glass of brandy in his hand, Hudson watched the three men in the potato field.

His stock was back in the corrals. That downy-cheeked lieutenant from the fort had brought them in, along with the weapons Hudson and his men had been forced to throw down. Of course he had had six filthy-looking soldiers to do the job for him. That made quite a difference. Hudson had been forced to depend on two scared Mexicans, who had failed him.

Lieutenant Merriam, the young fool, had not bothered to shoot the thief.

Hudson sipped his brandy. He had to get his mind off petty things and give it the range it deserved. After a time he was back to his great dream.

There were unlimited possibilities here. Things were not quite as he had visioned them in Virginia, but he was learning to shift his thinking to fit the country.

Water was a problem, for one thing. It did not always flow in the most convenient places. Such things as that could be changed, of course. The greatest difficulty was the scarcity of intelligent men to do his bidding. He might have been better off if he had brought one or two good overseers and fifty slaves with him.

But no, that would not have worked out well. White men quickly developed a crazy sense of independence and equality in this land, and the slaves most likely would have died from the cold winters.

Strangely, Hudson was not unhappy with what he had accomplished so far. He himself had done some of the work with his own hands, and, surprisingly, there had been a sort of pleasure in it, even though his whole thinking and breeding rejected the idea of a gentleman working. What he had held in mind all the time, and the idea was still soundly fixed, was the sort of feudal empire he had heard a traveler describe back in Virginia.

The man had talked of a huge place where he had been a guest for several weeks. A grant it was called. The main house and other buildings ran on without end. The tables were decked with snowy linen. Visitors dined from golden plates imported from Europe, drank the finest wines, sat on shaded porches and watched exhibitions of horsemanship. Hundreds of Mexicans worked on the far flung acres, taking care of cattle, horses, sheep, tending fields, running wineries. There was an ice house.

It was an establishment that put a paltry plantation to shame.

In the middle of all the economy and social life sat the owner, dispensing favors, giving orders to various respectful overseers, wise, respected, living like a king. That was the kind of life Hudson had been thinking of when he left Virginia.

He had not given up the idea. The land was here, miles upon miles of it. He still had gold in the house, although far less than when he had started west. The ambition was still with him, or at least the wish. His greatest lack still was trusted, competent men to carry out his orders. He had some position here. He was called Señor Hudson, except by frontier off-scourings such as the men who had stolen his stock, and those other two tramps.

Even Lieutenant Merriam, who hardly

counted higher than the wild trappers, looked on Hudson with some respect. Merriam's father ran a sawmill somewhere in Indiana. A sawmill! And the young idiot presumed to make moon eyes at Gail.

Hudson finished his drink and poured another. He was no drunkard and never had been. It was just that at times he liked the glowing feeling of self-respect that he achieved under the warmth of brandy.

It was unfortunate that there were no great landowners in the immediate area with whom he could visit, discuss problems, and from whom he could get advice. It was time Gail was married.

A union of houses, the Hudsons of Virginia with a noble Spanish family, would be a splendid move.

The brandy was stickily warm. Damn it, he should have an ice house. The Lord knew it was cold enough here in winter. He stared disgustedly at the Mexicans in the field. They were barefooted but they wore big silver spurs strapped to their heels, and they didn't give a damn about hoeing potatoes. If he understood enough of their language, he could make them hop. Diaz Escobar could. Sometimes.

Hudson scowled when he saw the rider coming. He started to reach for his rifle leaning against a tree, and then he noticed that the men in the field were not disturbed by the man's approach.

The rider was big and squat. He was smiling when he came into the grove, a flat-featured, ugly man making himself agreeable. Hudson thought he must have seen him somewhere before but he could not remember. At least he had some manners, strange as they were in this country: he did not dismount until Hudson asked him to.

The man removed his dusty hat. He made a bow of a sort and a shaft of sunlight striking through the trees shone on his shock of greasy, tumbled curls. He spoke slowly in Spanish and Hudson caught enough of it to understand that his name was Aragon. After that Aragon spoke more rapidly, gesturing toward the men in the field, pointing around the ranch, looking toward the cabin where Hudson's Mexicans lived.

"Gail, come here!" Hudson called. She had a fair working knowledge of Spanish. She had even picked up a little Ute and Apache. Hudson had studied Greek and Latin at the university and could still quote whole stretches of it, but it had seemed like losing dignity to learn an inferior language such as Spanish when Diaz Escobar could speak enough English to allow Hudson to give orders with a minimum of strain.

Gail came from the house and walked to the chair, standing behind her father. Aragon swept her a low bow, his face grave and respectful.

"See what he wants," Hudson directed.

Aragon and Hudson's daughter talked back and forth. "He wants to work here for you," Gail said. "He lives on the Huerfano. He says he knows a great deal about cattle and sheep."

"Well, by God. That's twice as much as any of the others know." Hudson liked Aragon's looks; there was hardness and determination behind the man's obsequious manner. Hudson spoke to him in English, "Could you make those men down there in the field move a little faster?"

"Señor?" Aragon looked blank. He spread his hands. Gail repeated the question in Spanish. "*Si*, Señor Hudson, *si!*" Flat cruelty spread across Aragon's eyes.

"Ask him if he knows Diaz and Bernal."

Aragon knew them. He shrugged. He said Bernal and Diaz Escobar were good men but lazy unless watched closely. They were also inclined to cheat and lie a little.

Hudson was pleased. "He knows them all right." Perhaps here in this squat man with the cruel eyes was the beginning of success.

"Tell him to go to the field. I'll watch and see what he can do with those men. Tell him if I like his methods, I'll hire him as overseer."

Gail hesitated. "That would be a mistake."

"Do as I say!"

They watched Aragon stride toward the field. *Now, that is the way a man should carry out orders,* Hudson thought, *instead of staring at you stupidly and scratching his fleas.*

Roman Aragon recognized the face of opportunity. He had come to the Hudson ranch seeking a job of any kind. None of Hudson's riders paid great attention to his orders, unless it was Diaz Escobar. They did as they pleased. That fact was known.

To have work here would make things much easier for Aragon. There was another man watching the dunes, the one who had worn moccasins, but he was not an Indian. One man was not too many but he was still a bad threat, particularly if he knew Aragon was also looking for the gold.

A smart man could spend most of his time close to the dunes while he was working for Señor Hudson. It was known that José Sanchez and his two cousins there in the field went to Conejos or to Costilla to visit as they pleased. Señor Hudson did nothing about that.

Hudson's proposal had startled Aragon, but in an instant Aragon had seen the tremendous chance he had never dreamed of. To be in charge of all the riders would make things very easy.

He strode into the field and looked at the three men leaning on their hoes. José Sanchez he knew. "I am now in charge here. Señor Hudson has ordered it. There will be more work done."

Sanchez looked at his cousins, grinning. "See who talks. I —"

Aragon was on him like a great cat. He bore Sanchez to the ground and they slid across the handle of the hoe, threshing among the young vines. Aragon slashed the point of his knife through the air an inch away from Sanchez's throat. The man tried to press the back of his head deeper into the soil. Aragon pricked him lightly in the throat with the knife.

He was watching the other two. They stood unsure for a moment and then they started to draw knives. Aragon leaped up with his blade flashing. The two men fell back. Their hands went back to the handles of the hoes.

In one quick moment Aragon knew he had put fear into all three of them. Work was something else. They would work while he was watching them, but at the first chance they were likely to get their horses and leave. That was not Aragon's problem.

"Work!" he said, holding the knife before him with the blade up.

Sanchez got off the ground. He picked up his hoe. The three men began to work steadily.

"Ah, that is better," Aragon said. "Pay now for some of the cheating you have done to Señor Hudson." He flipped his knife into the air and caught it by the handle. It had cost him many a gash before he had mastered that trick after watching trappers do it.

He swaggered back toward the grove.

Hudson said to Gail, "I've found a man."

"You've found a brute. I wouldn't trust him from here to the spring."

"Why must you criticize everything I do? You're worse than your mother!"

Gail walked back to the house without a word.

Aragon approached with an air of humility. He had gauged this weak man correctly. Flatter him, bow before him, move quickly when he gave orders, and everything would be just as Roman Aragon wished it.

"You're hired," Hudson said. He saw that Aragon did not understand. Hudson nodded. *"Bueno, bueno."*

"Gracias, Señor Hudson." Aragon held his hat in his hands. He said, "I will go now to look for your cattle." He waved his hands toward the mountains near the dunes.

Hudson caught the word "cattle" and repeated it. Damn it, why hadn't Gail stayed with him?

Aragon got on his horse and started away. From the doorway Gail called, "He says he's going out to look for the cows."

"Good!" Hudson said. At last he had someone around the place who was taking hold of things. He waved Aragon on.

After a time the feel of Gail's cold disapproval of the whole affair was like a physical force, but when Hudson turned irritably to look at his daughter, she was gone. He inched lower in his chair. He stared at the vastness before him with hypnotic fascination.

A magnificent house with white pillars rose among the trees. He was sitting on the porch of it. Riders dashed in and out of the yard and his lieutenants gave them orders. The mountains were teeming with his cattle and scores of brown riders watched after them. The field before him stretched out toward San Luis Lake, becoming one great run of rich greenness.

He poured a small drink. A cold fact disturbed him: his supply of brandy was almost gone. He would have to inquire of Aragon about the distillery in Taos. No doubt until later he would have to make a concession to the country and drink whisky.

Hiring Aragon had been a strong, sure move. From now on responsibility would not weigh so heavily.

Hudson mused contentedly, overlooking the fact that the three Mexicans in the potato field had slowed down.

CHAPTER TWELVE

The ride beside the dunes was the longest part of the whole trip for Rainbolt. It was windless. Heat waves bent up from the ground like vapor. The delicate coloring of the dunes changed before Rainbolt's gaze, fading, merging into one shade. Sometimes he saw tremendous hollows, curving down from the hairline crests of ridges, and then the coloring changed and the hollows looked like mounds. Except for the thin dark lines along the tops of some of the ridges, there was no sharp contrast anywhere in the masses of sand.

It flowed and changed at will, and yet Rainbolt knew it was always the same.

Sometime before he had put his pistol away, but that was only a temporary concession to logic: the weapon had been almost too hot to hold in a sweating hand.

Shaun was looking everywhere by habit, squinting far ahead, watching the rabbit brush and sage on their right, peering with a rifle stare at groves of cottonwoods and scattered clumps of piñons. Now and then he cocked his head and looked at the dunes.

"What caused them?" Rainbolt asked.

Shaun shook his head. "The Indians say they were always here."

The dunes had not been here always, Rainbolt thought, but they were here now, and he and Shaun were riding the edges of them and they were nearing the southern end. Rainbolt felt a tightening inside him.

He saw the broad gulch that must have held in bygone times the run of Medano Creek before the sand came and choked the stream to death. He saw the smoke gray pine tree on the mountains and beyond that, standing like a scar on the mountain, the gray rocks. He wanted to gallop toward the cottonwood.

Shaun rode slowly, his face dark with a moody kind of sullenness.

"Where's your man McCracken?" Rainbolt asked.

"I ain't thinking he's give up."

The dormant flame of suspicion leaped in Rainbolt. Suppose there had been some minor change in the hollow, and Shaun's six hundred and ten steps led them to nothing. Then Shaun could say that someone had found the gold.

Rainbolt put his hand on the butt of his pistol.

"I got a feeling we're being watched," Shaun said. His rifle swung across Rainbolt as Shaun changed its position.

Rainbolt saw the green-edged mark of a spring among the piñons and junipers on the skirts of the mountain straight ahead. His gaze swept over the pines above on the steep slopes. Suddenly he shared some of Shaun's uneasiness; everything was too calm and peaceful.

"We can't help it if we *are* watched," Rainbolt said. "Let's get the stuff and get across the hill." It was late afternoon.

"Not Mosca," Shaun said. "I don't want anyone between me and the top. We'll go back up the valley and pick another pass, and not the one we came across yesterday."

They stopped at the lightning-blasted cottonwood. Shaun's movements were easy but his eyes were intent as he dismounted, looking into the trees along the gulch.

Rainbolt saw the low ridge they had crossed to reach the cove. Beyond it, as before, all was brown where the steep slopes at the far side of the hollow rose. In the rippled shallow sand between them and the gold was nothing but the mark of the wind. He licked dust from his lips, watching Shaun narrowly.

Shaun looked to the priming of his rifle. "Sand changes some. Might take us longer to get the gold than it did to hide it, so —"

"What do you mean?"

"I mean we don't want to make everything as clear as tracks through a mud bank. Go out there maybe a couple hundred steps. Wander around from side to side like you didn't know where you was going." Shaun broke a small limb from the cottonwood. "Somewhere in line with the marks, drop this stick and then go on crooked-like some more. Stop about a hundred feet from the stick with your left leg lining up with the stick and the other marks."

Rainbolt considered the plan until he reasoned out the sense of it. He rode out on the sand until it began to deepen. He dismounted and walked. His course made long S marks that sloughed in behind him, but there was still a visible trail. He dropped the stick in line with the crotch in the tree, the dead pine, and the gray rocks. He walked on in an erratic pattern until he estimated he was far enough from the stick to make Shaun's sighting line accurate.

He stopped and came around, facing Shaun. He moved off to his left until, as nearly as he could tell, his left leg was lined with all the other reference points.

Shaun walked across the sand slowly, leading his horse and the pack mule. He varied little from a straight line, Rainbolt observed, but he did not seem to be pacing distance. Now and then Shaun stopped to look at the dunes. Once he went back to fiddle with something on his saddle, but when he resumed walking he was again coming on a true course.

A light wind was running. Rainbolt saw the tracks from the gulch smoothing away.

By the time Shaun came up to him, still walking without haste, the stick was covered. They did not need it any longer anyway; they had the sighting marks beyond it.

"You sure you got it right?" Rainbolt asked.

"Sure."

"You didn't lose count going back to your horse?"

"No."

"How many steps to here?"

"Two hundred and eighty-two," Shaun said.

"Stand still. I'll go on and stand in line with the marks again."

"Go ahead," Shaun said.

Rainbolt plunged on in the sand. His horse did not like the slippery weight around its legs. It followed him in short lunges. Rainbolt did not count his steps but after a time he thought he should have crossed the low ridge on the south side of the cove. There was the fine tracery of a ridge top there, swirling away into the deceptive brownness above.

He looked back. He was only a few steps off the true line. He moved over to guide Shaun, and while Shaun was coming on, Rainbolt looked behind him and all around him and felt sickening frustration.

There was no longer any hollow here. He was standing on deep sand that led upward and upward until it made a curve against the steeper slopes that had been the north side of the hollow.

He looked right and left, with the sickness turning into rage. For a moment he did not want to trust the reference points that he himself had made so sure of when they cached the gold, but the cottonwood had not changed and the mountains had not changed.

Only the treacherous sands had changed. Where there had been a hollow there was now thirty feet of smooth, brown sand covering the rocks, covering the sparse vegetation that had seemed such proof of stability.

Shaun's expression was fixed and wary when he came up to Rainbolt. They stared at each other.

"It's buried deep now, damn you!" Rainbolt said.

"Appears so."

Shaun was taking it too easy to suit Rainbolt.

"We'll get it out anyway," Rainbolt said.

"In this sand?" Shaun shook his head. "It runs like water. The wind maybe will uncover it again some day. We never will."

"That's what you'd like me to think, ain't it?"

"That's the truth, that's all," Shaun said. Except for his steady expression, he seemed relieved, as if he had just won an important victory.

"Is the gold down there?" Rainbolt asked softly. He was white. The words came past his cracked lips in a hiss.

"Where else could it be?"

"I don't know. Some of your Mexican friends from the Huerfano — How do I know but what —"

"I don't want to kill you." Shaun was never more dangerous than when his honesty had been questioned. "I will if you call me a liar again." Sweat lay in a ring around the strong cords of his neck. His shaggy black hair was pale with dust. His eyes were honed down to pinpoints of savagery. He had lived by simple rules and few of them, but those few were part of him.

"Go on," he said, "give me one more sight. I'll show you exactly where the gold lies."

Rainbolt looked at Shaun and still did not know whether to believe him or not, but he turned and went on up the slope. It was steeper than he had thought. His horse labored as he dragged it with him.

Shaun came on, his lips moving slowly as he counted. He stopped and looked back and was satisfied. "Down there," he said, looking where his feet were buried in the sand. "Down there where you found that damned piece of armor."

It was closer to fifty feet than thirty, Rainbolt guessed. "You knew the wind would cover it up!"

"No. There was rock in the hollow. There was grass. I didn't know."

"How do we reach it?"

"We don't. It's gone."

"Not as long as I'm alive it ain't gone!"

"Don't act crazy, boy. Let's get out of here."

"And leave that gold? It's only fifty feet down there!"

"It's the longest fifty feet God ever created," Shaun said quietly.

"You act like you don't care."

"I don't. That gold bothered me from the time we dug it. It put a spell on me and tried to get me killed. It's used gold. We killed men over it." Shaun looked off toward the San Juan. "I thought of a hundred things I was going to do with my share." He smiled. "Now I don't have to fret another minute about it. Let's go."

There was trickery in this. It was like the dunes singing their song when Shaun and Rainbolt had been burying the sacks; there was something waiting and treacherous that Rainbolt had not understood.

His rifle butt was sunk into the sand. He started to flip the weapon up to cover Shaun. This final move, long in his mind before he acted on it, should have been a quick and simple thing, but Shaun had not been blind since the night they started back after the gold.

He knocked Rainbolt's rifle aside with his own weapon before it was fully up. He crashed into Rainbolt and bore him into the sand. They rolled under the belly of the mule and the mule twisted away, humping its back as it fought the unstable footing. Rainbolt tried to draw his knife.

It was not like the fight they had had the first time they met. That one had started in fun. This one was savagery from the first movement.

Shaun would have broken Rainbolt's wrist if Rainbolt had not dropped the knife and jabbed the fingers of his free hand at Shaun's eyes. Every offensive move they made was aimed to disable or to kill. Shaun got one hand on Rainbolt's throat and Rainbolt kneed him in the groin to break the grip.

They fought through the sand, stumbling against each other, each giving the other no chance to get at his weapons, trying to kill each other with their bare hands. Neither knew anything about using his fists. It was butt and gouge and choke.

Rainbolt thought he was the stronger man, but in these fleeting moments he learned of the power in Shaun's tough old frame. Shaun fought with his legs, with his elbows, with his head. He butted Rainbolt in the face. Rainbolt tried to kick Shaun's legs from under him, but the sand was too deep and Shaun was too well set.

Rainbolt got his hand on his pistol, and Shaun caught his arm with a leverage that made the shoulder joint grate before Rainbolt could break away.

Shaun tripped him. They dropped into the sand, rolling over, each trying to slam handfuls of the grit into the other's eyes. There was scarcely any need to try; they were both half blinded as it was.

Rainbolt discovered one trick of leg wrestling he did not know. Shaun used both his legs to entwine one of Rainbolt's, and at the same time, sprawled almost crosswise on top of Rainbolt, caught Rainbolt's right arm with both hands.

Rainbolt tried to roll the wrong way, away from Shaun, instead of into him. The next instant Shaun's legs let loose. He drew them under him and used the solid platform of Rainbolt's body to leap like a frog. His knees came crashing down in Rainbolt's stomach. He gripped Rainbolt's throat and drove his head into the sand until it filled Rainbolt's ears.

The iron grip on his throat, the smothering feeling of sand growing higher around his head, gave Rainbolt the desperation to kick and thresh and arch his back in a tremendous effort to throw Shaun off. He might have done it with a lighter man. He failed with Shaun; and after the furious effort, Rainbolt had nothing left.

Shaun needed only one hand on his throat then. Shaun drew his knife. Rainbolt saw him but dimly. Shaun raised the knife. It stopped. The stain of brutality and lust began to leave Shaun's features. He growled something that was a sound with no words to it. He stood up and backed away.

"That gold didn't shine for me at no time," he said. He grabbed the short rope on the nose hitch of his horse and walked away with it and the mule. Rainbolt crawled to his rifle. He could hardly see but after a time he got the sights on Shaun's back.

The way Shaun was going, not looking back, not trying to keep the animals between him and Rainbolt, steadied Rainbolt and drove sanity into him. He lowered the rifle.

At the cottonwood Shaun unloaded the mule. Rainbolt saw him throwing equipment around, and then Shaun put some of it back on the mule and rode toward the Hudson ranch.

Rainbolt kept blinking his eyes and wiping the sand from the corners. His hat was lying where it had fallen during the fight. He pushed it down into the sand and left it as a marker, and went back to the cottonwood. Shaun had left him half of the camping outfit.

Could any man make the simple declaration that the gold did not shine for him, and ride away and leave it? Everything that Rainbolt knew about Shaun said that it could be; but still he was not satisfied.

His first idea had been that Shaun had sent one of his Mexican friends back across the pass to recover the gold while he and Rainbolt were staying on the Huerfano. Shaun must have known about the wind. He had stalled to let it cover his own duplicity.

The theory would not hold with Rainbolt. Somewhere deep in his being he knew, but would not admit, that Shaun had indeed ridden away and left the gold. It was still in the dunes. Why would he have shared it with someone on the Huerfano, rather than his own partner?

Still, Rainbolt wanted to be as sure as possible. If Shaun stopped at the Hudson place, then maybe he was not leaving the dunes for good.

Rainbolt bundled up the gear and rode toward the ranch at the big springs.

Long before he was there, he saw the dust of two animals going toward the far blue mountains. Shaun? Rainbolt watched the dust go on and on in a steady line across the valley.

He was still distrustful. He went into the ranch from the backside of the cottonwoods. The sorrels were in the corrals and the mules were there too. He dismounted and went toward the house. Mexicans were cooking their supper in the cabin away from the main building. Two of them peered out at him.

"Who visits here?" Rainbolt asked.

The Mexicans shook their heads. One of them pointed out toward the valley. "A man with a brown horse and with a pack mule passed, but not close to here."

Then it *was* Shaun. Rainbolt nodded toward the corrals. "They were stolen." It was a question.

One of the Mexicans said, "The soldiers brought them back."

Rainbolt went on into the yard of the house. Hudson was sleeping in a high-backed rawhide chair, an empty bottle on the ground beside him.

Rainbolt went past him, out to the edge of the trees where he had an unobstructed view of the valley. It was too dusky now to see much beyond the fence at Hudson's potato field, but Rainbolt stood there sensing the vastness of the valley, wondering about Shaun. He might have been all wrong about Shaun, after all. Maybe Shaun really didn't care about the gold.

It was hard to believe but it must be so.

When he turned back into the yard the man in the chair had stirred. "Who are you?"

Rainbolt went close to Hudson and then he saw that Hudson had been holding a rifle on him. "Jim Rainbolt," he answered.

"Oh!" Hudson said. "Now I remember you." He lowered the rifle, yawning. "Did you come across the pass today?"

"I crossed the mountains yesterday, yes."

"I was wondering if you saw anything of my cattle. I sent my overseer and two men out to scout around today."

"I didn't see any cattle." Rainbolt glanced toward the house. He saw Gail move across a lighted window. "Did any of the men who took your horses come back here?"

A stiffness came into Hudson's voice. "No. I recovered the stock at Antelope Springs the day after it was stolen."

"One man?"

Hudson hesitated. "Yes."

"Kill him?"

"We let him go," Hudson said curtly. "Why are you so interested?"

"He was one of a bunch my partner and me had trouble with." Rainbolt started away.

"You plan to camp here tonight?"

"No."

Gail was standing in the doorway. She stepped outside and away from the doorway so that the light fell directly on Rainbolt. Out of courtesy he paused and said good evening.

"You look like you've had a hard ride," Gail said. "I was just going to call my father to supper. You're welcome to stay and eat with us."

Rainbolt looked into the shadows beyond the house.

"Your friend too, of course, Mr. Rainbolt."

"He's gone." Rainbolt suddenly realized how hungry he was. He had not eaten since breakfast. He was tired and dusty. He tried to see Gail closely but the light was behind her and directly in his face. He smelled the clean, tantalizing odor of her and he sensed the loneliness in her.

It would be a pleasure to knock some of the dust from his clothes, to wash in the spring overflow, and to sit down to a meal inside the house. He rejected the whole idea. The gold came first. It was deep under the sand but it would not be safe unless he was close to watch the dunes.

Rainbolt said, "Thank you kindly, Miss Hudson, but I have to ride a little farther tonight."

"You look like you've ridden far enough."

"Good night," Rainbolt said, and walked away.

He must get back to the dunes at once. He would camp where he had seen the spring on the hillside. He would watch the sand. He would devise some means of uncovering his wealth. It was *all* his now.

Hudson came up to his daughter. "I have told you before about inviting these wild people into our home to eat. To talk to them a few minutes, yes. I can learn things from them that I need to know, but I won't have barbarians sitting at my table."

"He looked so tired, so worried about something."

"He looked like a man, you mean. You're getting too much like your mother, Gail. You begged that man to come inside."

"Yes. I would have liked to talk to him. We're not living in Virginia, you know."

"We'll be far greater here than we ever were there."

Hudson stepped inside and put his rifle over the doorway. The act always gave him a feeling of security, a feeling that he was a pioneer. He repeated his words about the greatness ready for them here in this new land. "Bear that in mind, Gail, and act accordingly. Keep these women-hungry men at a distance."

"Supper is ready." Gail turned away.

Hudson ate with good appetite. He was a healthy man who could, when necessary, bear up well under physical hardships, as he had discovered when bringing his wagons across plains to the mouth of the Fountain. After the meal he took one small glass of brandy.

Today he had made an excellent move in hiring Aragon as overseer. As soon as possible he would expand his crew, reaching out, building. . . .

"I wonder why he came back?" Gail said.

His dream interrupted, Hudson asked with annoyance, "Who?"

"Mr. Rainbolt, the man who was here tonight. Do you think that was really gold he and his partner had on the little spotted pony?"

"It was heavy enough." Hudson frowned. A pair of ignorant trappers with gold enough to make a horse sway-backed. Of course it had been gold or that group of cutthroats would not have been after them.

"Where was the other man tonight?" Hudson asked. "The old one who was so dirty and surly?"

"Mr. Rainbolt said he wasn't along."

Most travelers who came by were an inferior kind of annoyance to Hudson, but now his interest in Rainbolt and the older trapper was suddenly keen.

Their horses had been even more worn than those of the five men who came afterward. Hudson remembered how the little calico had plodded wearily toward the spring, although there was no great bulk upon it. Could the scraggly brute have carried that weight across the pass, with the fresh sorrels and mules hammering after it?

"Did Rainbolt say his partner had been killed?" Hudson asked.

"No. Just that he wasn't along."

With no firm idea in mind, but fascinated by the thought that there might be a large amount of gold only a few miles away, Hudson considered what possession of it would mean to his plans. At first it was only wishful thinking; but the thought kept growing until the obvious unfairness of uncouth trappers having a fortune they would squander, while a man with plans and intelligence had little to realize a magnificent dream, took hold of Hudson and enraged him.

Unconsciously he found himself staring at the rifle over the doorway.

He heard riders coming into the grove. One of them hailed the house. It was Aragon, who must have found lazy Bernal and Diaz somewhere in the mountains.

Aragon. He was a shrewd man but not very smart. Without arousing his suspicions, Hudson could use him to find out what had happened to the gold the two trappers had carried on the calico. Something must have happened to it, or else Rainbolt would be far away by now.

CHAPTER THIRTEEN

Roman Aragon returned to the ranch with a great show of importance. He had found Bernal and Diaz Escobar bringing in six cows with calves and he had made them turn them loose in the aspens not far above the dunes. Tomorrow, or whenever necessary, Aragon would take credit for finding the cows, even bringing them to the ranch if his new plan did not turn out well.

He gave loud and unnecessary orders to the Escobars about taking care of their horses, all this to impress Señor Hudson. He went to the door of the house, removing his hat, to make a report to Hudson. Once a muleteer with wagon trains between Independence and Santa Fe, Aragon could speak an intelligible brand of English, but he often found great advantage in not doing so.

When Hudson came to the door Aragon began to give his version of the day's work in Spanish.

"Come inside."

Aragon raised his brows politely. Hudson motioned with his arm, which was understandable in any language, and he called for his daughter.

Aragon told his story and Gail translated.

"It is as I suspected," Aragon said. "Because of the laziness of the men who work for you, your fine cows are scattered everywhere. However, after much hard riding today, I found several of them and know where there are more." The last statement held truth that amused Aragon, but he kept a respectful expression. The señorita was sharp and cold; she did not like him.

Hudson inquired about the number of cows Aragon had found and where they were, but Aragon could tell that he was not really greatly interested.

"A man came here this evening," Hudson said, "a tall trapper who was here before. His name is Rainbolt. He came for no reason and went away soon. Did you see him today?"

Aragon looked blank. He shook his head. "I was far in the mountains, searching hard." He had been in the piñons when Shaun and Rainbolt came to the dunes.

He had been cleverly hidden, waiting for them to get the gold and start back over the pass. His weapons were laid out so that he could kill them both when they came past him. Shaun and Rainbolt had acted in a strange way, going out on the dunes as though they did not remember where they had left the gold.

They had fought. Shaun went away. Then afterward the other one had ridden away. They had not dug or probed into the sand or tried in any manner to find their gold; but still they had taken their horses and the mule out upon the sands a great distance. It must be that the sand had changed, confusing their memories, or perhaps they suspected that they were being watched. They had ridden away without the gold, and the one called Shaun had made dust far out in the valley.

"I did not see the man," Aragon said. He observed that the woman was watching him with distrust.

"You said you live on the Huerfano. Didn't you see the two men when they came there?" It was a shrewd question, for Hudson did not know where the two trappers had gone after they left here.

Aragon appreciated its shrewdness. Hudson was not as stupid as he had thought. "I saw them, yes. They came with a spotted packhorse and there was, the people said, a great fortune on it, although this I do not know for truth." He gave his bland explanation to Gail and watched her as she spoke in English to her father.

Hudson said, "You know, Gail, those two may have deceived those ignorant Mexicans across the pass, but I doubt very much that they had the gold when they reached the Huerfano. Why did they come back, if they did?"

"Why are you so interested?"

"I'm not, really," Hudson said quickly. "Just a little curious."

The Señor Hudson was too curious. Aragon realized that he had underestimated him because he knew so little of living in this country, but when there was gold close by, all men's wits sharpened. Already there was one man watching the dunes, perhaps one of the trappers who had chased Shaun and Rainbolt. That was not good. If the gold was still there, Shaun and Rainbolt would be near by also. Aragon was now alone against them. He made a quick decision.

He said to Gail, "Ask your father if there is more he wishes to know about the cows."

Hudson had no more questions. Aragon started out. At the door he said, "There is a matter about the horses in the corral which I would like to show your father. Ask him if he will come to see. If so, Diaz can talk for me."

When he had the request, Hudson gave Aragon a long stare. He walked out into the darkness with him, past the cabin where the riders lived. Diaz came out to protest the hiring of Aragon, but Hudson waved him back curtly and told him that he would discuss the matter later.

Hudson and Aragon went on to the corrals. Aragon spoke in English then. "There is a strange thing happening at the dunes, Señor Hudson."

"Go on."

"It is said that you are a rich man. It is possible for a rich man to be even richer."

"I have often thought of that."

Aragon had no doubts now that he had made the right decision. All men were crazy for gold and Americans were the worst of all. "It may be that there is great wealth hidden under the sand, Señor Hudson."

"Perhaps it is gone by now."

"I do not think so," Aragon said. "You saw the weight the trappers had upon their packhorse when they were here?"

"Yes."

"It was not so when they were upon the pass later. I know. Was there a great wind here after they left your ranch?"

Hudson remembered back. About the time he was being robbed of his stock there had been a wind strong enough to bend the cottonwoods and knock dead branches from them; and it had blown heavily for several afternoons afterward. "Yes, we had wind."

"The sands change. I have seen them change myself."

"How much?"

"Greatly."

"Then maybe the gold is buried for good."

"No!" Aragon said. "The old man has been here many times before. He knows about the dunes. Would he be a fool and place it where it would be covered deeply? No, he would leave it somewhere along the edges where the sand does not change greatly."

"Then it's gone by now."

"The one called Rainbolt is still here. He fought with the other one. They parted. They have lied to each other, or they are confused about the place where the gold is hidden."

"Go on."

"There was much gold on the spotted horse?"

"There was a lot of weight, yes."

"It was gold. Was there enough for two of us?"

"Go on, Aragon."

"I have a plan." Aragon promptly gave it, and after a time Hudson returned to the house. There were details about Aragon's proposal that he did not like to dwell on, but the blame for them would be on Aragon's head. A man was a fool not to grasp opportunity with both hands when it loomed before him. Which was greater, a magnificent establishment here supporting hundreds of people, or the lives of one or two wandering trappers who might be killed by Indians before the leaves turned?

In darkness Rainbolt found his way to the spring he had observed on the hillside. The water seeped down along the bottom of a steep gulch. Where the moisture drifted away into sand at the mouth of the gulch, there was a level place. Many things were against it as a camping place — no cover at his back, the steep slopes on both sides, the dampness — but he could see out on the shoulder of the dunes, and he could hear if a horse came from the west.

He munched dried corn and drank from the trickle of water. Tied by a long rope to a juniper, his horse crunched grass along the sides of the seep. Rainbolt sat with his rifle, looking out upon the dunes.

A silver moon rose. The wide skirts of the dunes grew lighter and some of the slopes above caught the pale light, but in the hollows and curves of the dunes the shadows changed mysteriously. Rainbolt pulled his buffalo robe around him. He rested his back against a tree. His rifle grew heavy across his legs. A deer coming close on dainty feet to drink at the spring caught his scent. He saw the glow of its eyes as it looked at him, and then it spun away and went down into the cottonwoods.

The night wore on slowly. Shaun did not come. Rainbolt's mind began to shed the tensions of the day, of all the days since he had ridden up the pass, and he accepted at last that Shaun's going was final, that there had been no trickery in it, only something difficult to understand.

He kept watch on the dunes. The gold was there, and he could not let it go.

He dozed. Once he roused from a dream of seeing Spanish cavalrymen, with plumed helmets and shining breastplates riding toward him in a column of fours, riding hard and lightly down the dunes on beautiful horses. He stared across the night but there was nothing to see but the sand.

His horse had become entangled in the junipers. It thumped and crashed about and Rainbolt went to free it. He saw the first lightening of false dawn on the long swells of the sand when he went back to the mouth of the gulch.

By now, he thought, old Shaun was far away, resting well in his robe, free of the gold he had left so carelessly.

When light came it was time to build a

fire and eat, but Rainbolt had no time for that. He went down to the dead cottonwood, thinking to check the number of steps out to where he had left his hat. He would have to turn and sight behind him as he went, and his pacing would be obvious to anyone watching from the hills. And now, as Shaun had felt it, he had the feeling that eyes were on him.

Looking across the sand with a red-rimmed stare, he saw a dark object out where the hollow had been. It was his hat, the brim uncovered by the night wind. He went down the broad gulch to the west edge of the shallow sand and wandered out to his hat. He stirred around aimlessly on the sand, going in several directions, and then he returned to the hat and punched it back into the gritty softness with his feet.

He went straight down the bearing line, back to the cottonwood. It was, as Shaun had said, six hundred and ten steps.

For one brief moment Rainbolt thought of getting on his horse and leaving. He would find Shaun and they would sit together at a fire as they had done a thousand times, saying nothing, understanding each other well; and then gradually it would come about that one of them would say something about the gold and that would lead to something else said carelessly, and then they would laugh together about Rainbolt's stubbornness.

Rainbolt did not get on his horse and ride away. He went back to the spring and then he turned to look at the dunes. They mocked him and enraged him, but the men who had forced him to bury in the sand two hundred and fifty pounds of gold enraged him more, even though most of them were dead.

The dunes he could fight only with patience; if there were any of the men left, he would seek them out and kill them to ensure his own security during the wait that was ahead of him. Until that was done, there could be no rest for him.

After breakfast he would see if there was anyone else watching the dunes.

Green River had seen almost every move Shaun and Rainbolt had made since returning to the dunes. He was in the rocks high above the gulch. Day after day he had moved the two Ute ponies he had caught, taking them from one aspen pocket to another so that they could forage. He had killed a deer and made jerky of it and with that as his only food he had wolfed it out on the mountain.

After several days he was doubtful of the accuracy of his own guesses about the gold.

Mexicans from the ranch at the big springs had come and gone along the trail below him, but no one went near the dunes. Then one afternoon McCracken came, riding in from the west side of the dunes, going on up toward the pass. A man might have known that McCracken would not be fooled forever.

Green River's first thought was to join forces with him, but there was the matter of having run away from the falls that night. That same afternoon Shaun and Rainbolt arrived.

His breath coming fast and hard, Green River watched them go out on the sand. Shaun was taking the pack mule. They were going to get the gold. But something went wrong. They did not dig. They did not search at all. They got into one hell of a fight, threshing around in the sand; and for a time Green River was sure one had killed the other. He hoped it was so.

The furious dust settled and they were both all right.

In their haste to cache the gold they must have made a mistake, forgotten something, and the fight had been a result of their blaming each other for the error.

At any rate, they had not found the gold. It had to be in the dunes or they would not have gone out on them. They broke up, but now Rainbolt was back. Green River was right; the gold was down there. He was unable to make heads or tails of what Rainbolt was doing. It appeared that Rainbolt did not know himself.

Green River had suffered much and waited long. He could afford to wait longer, for that, obviously, was what Rainbolt was going to do. And McCracken. . . .

Green River caught glimpses of Rainbolt going on foot up the steep hills above the place where he had camped. The man might be stalking him, going high to gain the advantage, slipping along through the timber.

Then seven riders came from the west, kicking dust among the piñons and junipers. Green River recognized Hudson, and he recognized a squat figure on a blue roan horse. That was one of the Mexicans who had been past here twice. They were on their way to the pass. Everything was all right. But no, the whole bunch dismounted in the cottonwoods close to the sand.

Five of them went to work, the big Mexican directing as he waved his arms and shouted. They began to build a corral down there, lashing poles to trees, piling up dead cottonwoods. The whole world was invading the place! Green River cursed, for out on the sand the puddled marks of Rainbolt's wandering this morning were still visible.

Hudson rode his sorrel out on the sand, the animal bunching and kicking as it plowed along in the wake of Rainbolt's tracks. Hudson went out to the end of the tracks and came back, stopping beside a forked cottonwood that his men were using as one corner of the corral.

Things were getting too thick for Green River. He kept looking uneasily over his shoulder, up there where Rainbolt might be creeping down on him. Green River slipped away to look at his ponies. He never used the same route twice; he never stayed twice in the same place among the rocks.

The ponies were all right, except that they had run out of grass. Green River stood still, staring at the tracks of a man who had been here a short time before. He followed them for a short distance. Someone, Rainbolt undoubtedly, was back-trailing him to where he had just left.

He might not be the man Shaun was — there were only a few like old Shaun — but he was enough for Green River. The whole business was coming apart. Green River felt like running again, but he remembered the weight that had been on the packhorse. The gold was right here within easy reach, if only there weren't so many against him.

He wanted to run and he wanted to stay but he was not going to stay alone. He pushed down his fear of McCracken. He took the ponies and went to find him.

It was easier than Green River had hoped, and much more unexpected. He was following old tracks in the timber on a bench to the north of the pass trail. The pines stood tall and wide-spaced. The hoofs of his ponies made little noise on the needle mat. Now and then, looking back through lanes among the trees, Green River had a clear view of the dunes.

Suddenly a pleasant voice said, "Stand still, Green River." It was a moment before recognition came through shock and told Green River that McCracken had spoken.

He was lying off to the side in a shallow pit where the roots of a wind-felled tree had torn up the ground. "I've been looking all over hell for you, McCracken."

"I imagine. Where's the sorrels?"

Green River moistened his lips. All he could see of McCracken so far was the barrel of his rifle across a pitch-yellow root. "A bunch of soldiers got 'em away from me and took 'em back to Hudson."

"I noticed he had 'em again."

Green River walked toward the fallen tree

slowly. "I waited all that night for you, McCracken. You didn't come back, so I took the animals —"

"I figured you did."

"I waited all night!"

"Sure," McCracken drawled, "I'll bet you did."

"So help me God! Where've you been?"

McCracken did not answer. His silence and the rifle made Green River's belly squirm, but he kept on walking forward until suddenly McCracken rose and stood looking coldly at him. "The gold is in the dunes," Green River said. "They never had it when we ran 'em across the pass. It's down there in the dunes and they haven't got it yet."

"I know that."

"But do you know where it is?"

"Do you?"

"I've got an idea," Green River said.

"You have like hell. Shaun and Rainbolt couldn't find it, so how would you know where it was?"

"I've been watching —"

"So have I." McCracken turned his head. The pit was in line with a wide lane through the timber, looking straight down on the shoulder of the dunes and the cottonwoods where the Mexicans were working. "Do you know who that big wide Mexican is?"

"He works for Hudson."

"He didn't until the other day. That's Roman Aragon from the Huerfano. He never did anything but steal horses and kill traders. He was on the Huerfano when I went there after Shaun. What's he doing here now?"

"I don't know," Green River said. He was feeling more at ease.

"Somehow he's caught on about the gold, Green River. That corral is a fake. Why would they have a corral there?"

"Maybe they —"

"Maybe nothing. It's a fake and Hudson's in on it. He has to be. We can handle him and Aragon all right. The main worry is Rainbolt and Shaun."

Green River hid the elation the word *we* gave him. He was back in the game. "Shaun left," he said.

"I saw it all. He left but I don't trust him to stay away. Shaun kills when he fights, but he didn't kill Rainbolt. No matter what, he thinks too much of Rainbolt. One of these days he may come back here."

"We won't be here forever."

"It may be a long time. One of two things happened down there when they buried the gold, maybe some of both. They were in a hurry and didn't take their bearings; or else the wind shifted the sand. One way or another, Rainbolt has a fair idea of where it is."

"Rainbolt's trailing me right now."

McCracken shot a quick look through the trees. "Why didn't you say so when you first showed up?"

"He'll be a long time unwinding my trail."

"Don't be so sure." McCracken stepped out of the pit and looked all around him. "We've got to have Rainbolt alive. We've got to work on him and find out everything he knows about the cache."

"Apache methods?"

McCracken smiled. "The Apaches can't hold a candle to a Spaniard when it comes to making a man talk. I'll show you when we get him. He's got to watch everybody around the dunes. All we got to do is watch him. When the time's right we'll grab him."

"I know where his camp is."

"Don't you think I do? But it won't be in the same place tonight. Let him wear himself down. He'll fall asleep in spite of himself, and then we'll get him."

CHAPTER FOURTEEN

Lieutenant George Merriam stopped at the Hudson place on his way to a three-day scouting mission at the northern end of the valley. A report had come to the fort that Mano was moving a hundred Utes toward Poncha Pass. Colonel Columbine thought it well to keep an eye on them.

Keeping an eye on moving Utes was like watching desert mirages, but Merriam was grateful for orders that would let him see Gail Hudson on his way up the valley, and perhaps again on his return.

That was about all he was grateful for in the whole San Luis Valley. There was too much dust and heat and wind in the summer, and too much cold and wind in the winter. Fort Massachusetts was a hell of a place to live, so close to the hills that if the Indians got an idea, they could gobble it up.

He walked his ten men into the yard. They dismounted on order, and Lieutenant Merriam flipped his reins to Sergeant Mulligan, slapped dust from his gloves and hat, and went toward the house to talk to Gail. He was a chunky man with a blondness that did not take well to the hot summer sun. He walked with West Point correctness. He was only twenty-four.

She met him at the doorway with a smile. Her smile, so slow and sure, and maybe even amused, always unhinged some of his cockiness. "The Colonel sends his compliments, Miss Hudson. With your permission we'll water and rest for a few minutes."

"You're always welcome, Lieutenant."

"Thank you. Is your father at home?"

"He's gone out with the men to build a corral."

For what? Merriam wanted to ask. For cattle that he had forgotten for two years?

"I'll get you a cup of coffee," Gail said. "I've just made a fresh pot. Where are you going this time?"

"To the head of the valley. Probably no farther." Dust and sweat made an itching under the collar of Merriam's blouse. "I may get a transfer sometime this fall."

"That's good," Gail said coolly. "I know how much you've wanted it."

It was always that way. She knew what was in his mind, but she kept a distance between them. He drank his coffee and went out to the springs.

His men were resting in the shade. They still had time left of the promised fifteen minutes, but Merriam mounted them up and resumed the scout. He gave Gail a smile and a small salute as he passed. He guessed he never would be worth a damn when it came to talking straight out to a woman.

Gail watched the detail increase its pace after it left the grove. George Merriam was a solid, sturdy figure as he rode away.

Why not indeed marry him and go away from here? John Hudson could never change, and she would be of little help to him by staying here. Even now she was worried about something that he and Aragon were working on together. This morning she had seen them talking in the yard and it was obvious that Aragon could speak English, after all. She had heard them say something about Rainbolt as they walked away toward the corrals.

Rainbolt. He had been here twice. An unhandsome man, but the wildness of the country was somehow blended with a gentleness in him that appealed to Gail. He was a kind of man she had never known. In some ways he was like a savage, but there was no doubt that he was a man all the way through; and in leaving that first time, he had said things about her that still made her strangely restless and excited. . . .

★ ★ ★

Rainbolt stayed on Green River's trail until he developed the uneasy feeling that he was running into a trap. Since the day he and Shaun had buried their gold in the sand, Rainbolt had seldom been able to give complete concentration to any one job of the moment; part of him was always dragged down by worry over the gold. It was that way now.

Even as he followed Green River's trail, not knowing who the man was, some of the keenness that he needed was blunted by knowing that Hudson's men were building a corral six hundred and ten steps from the gold. They had even used the bearing tree as a corner.

Maybe chance had brought them to the place, but Rainbolt could not forget how sharply Hudson had eyed the panniers on the calico that night when Rainbolt and Shaun had ridden into his yard.

Fretting over the building of the corral, trying to keep from being surprised while trailing a man — all lowered Rainbolt's effectiveness. He came to a small bench where the pines stood far apart. He was halfway across it before he saw the faint disturbance of the needle mat where Green River had stopped and changed direction abruptly. He saw the spokelike roots of a fallen tree too late to have saved himself from ambush if there had been a man behind them.

His man was not there, but he had met another man and they had gone away together, back to the two unshod horses and then in a slow circle around the mountain.

Two of them now; Rainbolt's worry doubled. He followed uneasily for half an hour. then stopped. The longer he waited to find out about those two men, to kill them if necessary, the more complicated his guarding of the cache would be. Maybe he should continue on after them. But what was happening down at the dunes? He could not see from where he was in the timber. He had to watch everyone if he was going to protect the gold.

Rainbolt went back down the mountain.

For three days he played a deadly game of hide and seek with McCracken and Green River. They always faded away before his stalking, drawing him on until he knew they were setting traps for him. And then he would turn back, cursing himself but still clinging to Shaun's hard-taught caution.

Finally the corral was finished. Hudson's riders brought in a few calves and cows, branded them and turned them loose. Except at night, both Aragon and Hudson were always at the corral. Sometimes Rainbolt was sure they had seen him watching them from the hills; but they had never given any sign that they knew he was around. He himself had been close enough to the gulch one day to recognize Aragon, to know him as the uncle of the boy Rainbolt had taken down the Huerfano.

Hiding the gold had been a terrible mistake; no one had been fooled except for a short time. Only light winds ran across the dunes, making wavelets in the sand above the gold. And his memory of bare earth and scrubby grass that had been in the hollow only a short time before mocked Rainbolt as he kept his lone vigil.

He grew gaunt and savage. He moved his camp each day. There was only limited water along the hills south and west of the dunes, so his pattern of changing camp sites was restricted. He knew he would wear it thin before long and then his chances of getting the sleep he needed would be greatly decreased.

They were waiting, all of them, for him to make a move to uncover the gold. Perhaps they had not guessed yet how deeply it was hidden.

Rainbolt was waiting for the wind to do again what it had done before. But the wind was perverse now, blowing gently in the morning and evening, merely caressing the sand.

It came to Rainbolt at times how lonely and fiercely obsessed he was; but the realization began to be covered by a hatred of those who threatened the gold, by an unreasoning determination to protect at all costs what was his.

Three Utes rode by at dawn one day, seeming to rise from the valley floor with the coming of light. Rainbolt recognized one of them and went down from his hiding place to talk to them.

The Utes had seen old Shaun five days before. He was deep in the San Juan with Rico's band, loafing, hunting, living out the long days carelessly.

Rainbolt watched the Utes ride toward the pass. Once again he thought of leaving, of going away and forgetting that there ever had been two hundred and fifty pounds of gold in buckskin bags. But he went back to his camp at the spring where he had spent the first night. As he lifted his bearded face from drinking, water dripped into the bright pool. He kept staring until the surface of the spring was clear and then he saw a strange face peering at him.

The beard was matted. Strain was burned

across the high cheekbones, and the eyes were dark and savage.

A twig scratched on a juniper near by. Rainbolt whirled around with his rifle raised and his motion scared away the tiny gray bird that had made the sound.

He composed himself to watch the dunes. Waiting was all there was. One day the wind would blow again, slamming out of the southwest to undo its careless work. *It had to. . . .*

It did not come that day, nor the next day either. There did come a day when Rainbolt realized that no one had been near the corral for some time, and he had seen no fresh signs of the two men who had been keeping to the rocks and timber of the pass.

A group of Mexicans went toward the Huerfano. Small parties of dark Utes passed. A lone priest on a mule went by, his robe pulled up and tied around his waist, his muscular brown legs showing the dust of a long ride.

All those were normal travelers and none of them was interested in Rainbolt's dunes. Rainbolt began to discount some of his suspicion of Aragon and Hudson. After all, they had branded cows in the corrals, and they had not shown any undue interest in the dunes. Rainbolt did not drop them completely from his list of threats but he did put them off as the least of his dangers at the moment.

Beyond doubt the other two were McCracken and the man who had run away with the sorrels and the mules, Green River. Shaun had strong respect for McCracken; in fact, there were times when it seemed Shaun was a little afraid of McCracken, at least as much afraid as he ever was of any man. Shaun had said that McCracken would never quit.

Now Rainbolt had to agree.

He dozed in the daytime, stayed awake at nights. One night he scouted the Hudson ranch on the long chance that he could find out something about Aragon's knowledge of him. He went clear in to the stack of native hay that Hudson had cut and stored to feed his stock.

He heard the Mexicans in their cabin. Aragon was in the house with Hudson but presently he came out and went to the cabin with the others, and thereafter the Mexicans had little to say.

Rainbolt went back to his lonely camp. He was extra vigilant that night. For a long time the hat he had left out on the sand had been troubling him. Sometimes it was covered with sand and again the light wind took the sand away and left the dark brim showing as a small dot.

At daylight he went out to get the hat. Enough wind was running to cover his tracks, and he did not go in a direct line from the forked cottonwood. When he found the hat he took sightings at a right angle to the other bearing marks. He picked a juniper tree with a trim top, a greenish colored rock, and the point of a hill close to a shimmering alkali flat.

The intersection of the two lines of backsight was directly above the gold. When the wind came and began to bear the sand away, he would not have to step off paces to know where the gold lay.

His tracks slid into smoothness behind him as he went back to the gulch. There was wind, but not the powerful currents that were running the day he and Shaun first tumbled into the hollow.

During the long afternoon Rainbolt sat under a tree and dozed, watching the tawny play of the sun on the sand during his intervals of awareness. The dunes and the drowsy quiet worked a spell on him. He fell sound asleep.

It was the rattle of small stones that woke him. He was bringing up his rifle when two men grabbed him and he heard Mc-

Cracken's soft, unexcited voice: "Get his arm there."

A piñon club thumped against Rainbolt's head. He still tried to struggle. "Don't kill him, you fool," McCracken said. The club came down again.

He was belly down across a mule when he came to. His wrists and ankles were tied hard. McCracken and Green River took him to their camp in the aspens close to a small stream that Rainbolt knew must be Medano Creek.

They lifted him from the saddle and put him on the ground almost carefully.

"There's only one thing we want to know," McCracken said. "Where is the gold?"

Rainbolt stared up at them. Green River was grinning.

"That's the only time I'll ask," McCracken said in his pleasant voice.

He waited a moment. Rainbolt said nothing. Green River produced a bundle of pitch splinters and began to build a fire. For a while Rainbolt thought he knew what was coming, but Green River boiled coffee over the fire and he and McCracken shared it, drinking from the pot. They seemed to have forgotten Rainbolt.

McCracken filled his pipe with black tobacco and sat a few moments longer enjoying the smoke. He rose and stepped off into the aspens and came back with a bundle that dripped water. He began to spread it out. It was cow hide, freshly removed.

Rainbolt felt sweat breaking out on his chest and arms as the two men lifted him and wrapped him in the wet, stinking hide.

CHAPTER FIFTEEN

Paisano was the daughter of a Cheyenne woman and a Spanish trader, but this was of no importance to her. She was a woman of pride and also a woman in love. A man had lied to her, perhaps not because he wished to but because the strangeness of white blood made him lie. Americans were not as other people. They came from far places where customs were strange, so one had to forgive them much in order to get along with them.

Paisano had already forgiven Rainbolt for a great deal; she might forgive him his lie about returning to her — after she determined what had made him tell the lie.

Paisano was not going to wait for him to return; she would go find him. It was no secret on the Huerfano where he was, although it was said that Shaun was no longer with him. Near the end of the dunes across the mountains something strange was going on. It was so strange that it was said that Roman Aragon was working, which was something he had never done before.

Some of the people of the Huerfano whispered of gold, and some of the more adventuresome among them had gone across the mountains to see what was going on. None of them had liked what they had seen, although Paisano had only the gossip of the women to guide her in this, and so they had returned.

She was not concerned with gold. She was concerned with Rainbolt. She would go herself to see him. If he lied to her again, she would return and put him from her mind, although that would not be simple; and then perhaps she would marry José, Gondora's oldest son, whose wife had died two years ago.

Her mind made up, Paisano went to see Gondora. He listened well, this fierce little man who was her only father. Dimasio Gondora had been many places in his day. He told her how the Indian wives of trappers died of lung fever, or of pure shame and hopelessness, when their husbands brought them to St. Louis or Independence or other white man's towns on the great river across the plains. This, he said, was not what he wanted for Paisano.

Paisano lowered her head and said, "I wish to go find him."

"There is danger where he is. McCracken — you will remember him — surely killed the trader Gonzalo Sedeno, took his mules, and followed Shaun and Rainbolt when they left here. Even now he must be waiting at the dunes."

"I wish to go find Rainbolt."

"Roman Aragon now works for Señor Hudson, and they have built a corral close to the sand. My sons say —"

"I wish to go."

Gondora grunted. He thought for a time. "Go then. I will send three of my nephews —"

"I wish to go alone."

She was part Indian. That was the trouble, Gondora told himself. "Take with you Chico. He has been across the mountains. He will be of some use. Here all he does is eat my food and cause my grandsons to tell even bigger lies than usual." Gondora frowned. "The Utes ride back and forth across the mountains all summer."

"I speak their language."

"That will be of great help when they capture you and take you away to the far mountains by the River of Lost Ones."

"I am not afraid."

"Yes, that is the trouble." Gondora sighed. "What you need I will give you, and I will hope for your return."

"Thank you, Father."

Paisano and Chico rode up the pass together. For a time Chico chattered like a magpie. It was a grand excursion. In a sheath at his side he had a fine knife which his uncle had thought lost since last summer. He wished he had a big pistol also, but his uncle would not have believed that a pistol could be lost easily.

Chico was a protector. Of all the men of Gondora's household, Gondora had selected him to watch over Paisano.

They passed the place where the first dead man had lain until someone dumped him down into the pool at the bottom of the noisy falls. It was gloomy in the heavy timber. They went on up the rocky trail to the top and there was another dead man rotting in the sun. The odor was terrible. Chico held his breath.

Paisano rode on, her face serious as she watched the timber. When they passed the place where someone had rolled a third dead man down into the rocks below the trail, Chico wondered why he had thought this such a fine excursion.

They could see the pale brown of the distant sand dunes and the great valley with the blue mountains all around that teemed with Utes.

Chico kept his little pony close to the rump of Paisano's horse.

CHAPTER SIXTEEN

On the second day Rainbolt doubted that he could last much longer. The hide was around him from his armpits to his thighs, shrinking to flintlike hardness, slowly squeezing the life from him. His arms were outside, bloody and swollen where he fought the bindings on his wrists. From the rawhide on his wrists, thongs led to his knees, which were also lashed together. His ankles were bound and secured to a tree.

From his neck, rawhide thongs made a V to pegs in the ground. He could move his head a little by rolling it from side to side. They had put him on a bed of spruce boughs, not for comfort, but to allow the air to circulate evenly all around the hide.

For six hours each day the sun was on him. He no longer had any sweat to give.

Just once McCracken had asked about the gold.

They had Rainbolt's horse now. All his other possessions were hanging in trees or scattered around the camp. A half hour ago McCracken and Green River had gone away.

Once more Rainbolt tried to break the

thongs between his wrists and knees. He strained, rocking from side to side. Blood ran on his wrists. His knees were raw from rubbing them together. His neck ached because his head lay lower on the mat of boughs than his body. He sawed back and forth with all his strength until he felt the deadness growing in his arms again. White flashes crossed his brain as he held his breath.

When he gave up trying there was no relief because he could not take a deep breath. For a time he went completely out. As he came slowly back to consciousness, he heard his own rapid, shallow breathing. The insides of his upper arms were raw from rubbing on the hard, upcurled edges of the hide just below his neck. For a while his sweat had kept the cow hide from drying rapidly, but now there was nothing but burning heat under the covering.

How long could he last? There was no use in telling McCracken what he wanted to know. Rainbolt had seen too far behind the man's cold eyes to hope for any kind of mercy from him. Green River was weaker; but in his case weakness was the mother of cruelty.

Rainbolt stared at the sky. It was the same blue earthly cover he had seen all his life, but now there was a new and terrible meaning in it.

He felt the hard claws of black beetles working against his skin where the edges of the hide had curled away. The beetles and ants and other crawling things had been cleaning meat and blood from the hide ever since it had been about him. The first day, after McCracken and Green River stripped his shirt off and wrapped the hide against his bare chest, there had been some looseness because Rainbolt had struggled mightily to keep his chest inflated. After he was bound and left, the beetles had swarmed under the hide, scuttling, crawling, pushing their metallic claws against his skin until he wanted to scream.

Even now the memory of it made a cold wrinkling down Rainbolt's spine, as if wind were blowing there on sweat.

Ants straying up his pants legs made him shudder. The constriction around his chest was growing tighter. The hide would never break. It would go on shoving his ribs against his lungs, crushing him until he could no longer breathe. He might go mad. He feared that most.

Some parts of the hide dried faster than others, making ridges that felt like rocks pressing against him. The first day, when there was still flexibility in the hide, Rainbolt had tried to pull loose the stakes that held the rawhide around his neck. If he could have done that he could have bent forward enough to chew the rawhide on his wrists. But now, even if his head were free, the encasement around his chest had hardened so that he could not have sat up or doubled his body.

How long could he last? By lying quite still he would live longer than if he struggled. But there would be a greater chance that he might break and give satisfaction to his captors.

Slowly at first and then with increasing savageness he tried once more to break the bond between his wrists and knees. He felt something give. There was a little slack now. He used it to make jerking movements. The rawhide on his wrists grew tighter with each jerk until his fingers were so swollen that he could not move them.

The blackness came again. He returned to consciousness later to hear his breath wheezing in his throat. Insects were buzzing around him. Something was crawling on his lips. He rolled his head weakly against the spruce boughs.

Again he struggled; the result was the same. The terrible pressure around his chest increased until his head fell back and the relaxation of unconsciousness sent oxygen slowly back to his brain.

Once more he tried to break his bonds.

He was lying in a half stupor when he heard McCracken and Green River return to camp. Green River's voice was a dim murmur far away. "Look at that. He busted some of the rawhide." Rainbolt felt his arms dragged tight once more until his shoulder sockets burned with agony.

"He's a tough bastard," McCracken said. "Anybody that ran with Shaun would have to be. Give him some water."

"It'll make him sweat."

"That won't hurt the hide any now. In another two days it'll be like a chip."

Green River poured water on Rainbolt's face until Rainbolt choked and twisted away to keep from strangling. "You fool!" McCracken cried. "Give him a little at a time until he gets all he can hold."

Rainbolt drank until his stomach hurt. He felt nauseated then and had to fight to keep the water down. Green River built the boughs up under his head and left him. Thereafter, for all the attention the two men paid him, Rainbolt might have been a piece of camp equipment not needed at the moment.

It would be easier to bear if they taunted him and jeered, if they tried to extract his secret with shrewd questioning, for then he would have had something besides the hide to fight; but they ignored him.

Rainbolt tried to live it out minute by minute, but thoughts of the long night ahead began to work on him. The cold would increase the agony in his cramped muscles. By day there was the blue sky. By night there were the frosty stars and the chill wind blowing on him. Such sleep as he got was tortured with dreams of walking in long strides across meadow grass with a soft, warm wind against him.

Anything was worth a few breaths of air, a chance to let his muscles sag and relax. "Cut me loose."

It was only sunset.

Green River started to rise from where he was cooking at a fire. He looked inquiringly at McCracken, and McCracken motioned him back.

They want me to beg, Rainbolt thought. He would not do it. But a half hour later he heard his own voice cry out again. "Cut me loose!"

Chewing a piece of meat, McCracken walked over and looked down at him. "You know when you'll get loose." He waited for

Rainbolt to speak.

For the first time there was something for Rainbolt to match his stubborn will against. McCracken wanted him to talk, with the promise understood that he would be freed afterward. It was a lie. It would never be anything else. No matter what Rainbolt told him, McCracken would not free him. McCracken was waiting for him to break.

From hatred of the man and from stubbornness Rainbolt brought up strength. He stared up at McCracken and smiled.

McCracken watched him without emotion. He walked back to the fire slowly.

That night Rainbolt dreamed of Shaun. Shaun was creeping in on the two men sleeping in warm robes. Shaun was here. He would kill them both and then come running with his knife to slash the lacings on the hide.

Cold light came through the trees. Rainbolt watched Green River and McCracken get out of their robes. Green River sauntered over and looked at Rainbolt's bonds. He walked away, scratching his belly and yawning.

Before long the sun would be up. The hide would shrink some more.

After breakfast Green River went away from the camp. He returned an hour later and said, "They're back, Hudson and Aragon. Hudson's out there on the sand poking around with a pole."

"Let him poke. He won't get anywhere that way."

"Why won't he? He might get lucky."

"If he does, we'll go to the ranch. We took his horses once, didn't we?"

"I don't like that idea," Green River said. "Them soldiers were at the ranch again a few days back. They're always prowling around there. Hudson's got six Mexicans working for him now and they seem to be sticking close to home the last few days. The thing for us to do is find the gold and slip away without the whole country knowing about it."

"That's the best idea, yes," McCracken admitted. He walked over and looked down at Rainbolt. "How would it feel to take a real deep breath, Rainbolt?"

Rainbolt stared at him and tried to smile.

McCracken walked away. "We'll see how he feels this evening," he told Green River. "All right, let's go down closer and see what Hudson is stirring up with his pole."

Rainbolt ground his teeth together to keep from yelling for them to come back. He was not sure whether he had called out or not. The two men went away and the quiet of the forest held. Insects droned around him. Rainbolt's body was so leaden now that it was an effort to move his head to keep the insects off.

It hurt his eyes to watch the blue sky. He closed them and a vision came to him of standing in gentle rain on a creek in the San Juan. His body was cool and without pain. But the vision did not last long. The agony returned. Rainbolt groaned and fought to break loose.

Deep in the San Juan old Shaun Weymouth sat in a snug camp under spruce trees and watched rain seething into the beaver ponds below him. For some time he had been a discontented man. Four days before he had left the camp of some of his Ute friends because he knew that if he stayed longer he was going to quarrel with them.

His appetite was all right. His wounds had healed. He was in a country of abundant game. Yesterday, just for the hell of it, he had stood on a cliff and scared the daylights out of a grizzly bear eating grubs in a hollow log by throwing rocks at it and shouting insults.

Shaun was all right, except that he was miserable.

He had not run out on Rainbolt. You

didn't do such things to a partner when he was in a fix. You stayed with him and went under, if that was the way things turned out. But if your partner lost his senses and went plumb loony over something he could never have, no man was obliged to stick around and give him advice.

That was the way it was with Rainbolt. The gold had been hurting him from the day they found it. He had worried about someone getting it away from him before it was dug. His suspicions later that Shaun was trying to hog it all had been the worst thing about the whole mess; no other man in the whole world could have called Shaun the things Rainbolt had called him — and lived.

Rainbolt had completely lost his head over that gold.

Shaun stared from his shelter into the rain. Suddenly the storm was over. Wind began to break rifts of blue in the sky and the sun came out again, warming the soaked earth, sending light vapors up.

It was hard to say what made a man so stubbornly crazy about gold. In his younger days Shaun supposed he had been the same way as Rainbolt, but Shaun had spent a lifetime where gold was almost worthless. You couldn't load a rifle with it. You couldn't use it as salt on meat. You couldn't buy yourself out of a bad fix with the Indians if you had a cart load of it. Gold just didn't shine in the life Shaun had led.

Speaking for himself, he was glad the gold was where it likely never would be seen again. Things had gone better for him as soon as the gold was buried. He had even got out of a scrape that his feelings had said was going to be his last one.

Rainbolt did not know how Shaun had felt the day he came striding down the Huerfano, wounded, tired and hungry, but feeling wonderful because he had just beat something tougher than McCracken's bunch. Come to think on it, Shaun's reluctance to go back after the gold must have looked a little strange to Rainbolt. Maybe it had been reasonable for him to be full of suspicion.

Gold was like that. Back where Shaun had come from, men had killed each other over a danged sight less gold than was in the dunes.

Shaun began to have a sneaking hunch that he should have stayed on a while longer at the dunes. Maybe Rainbolt would have come to his senses. Maybe Shaun could have talked some reason into him after a time. But no, old Shaun Weymouth had let his Indian temper run sky-high. After the fight out on the sand he had waited a few minutes to see if Rainbolt would come on over to the cottonwood, and then had said to hell with him and ridden away.

It just might be that Shaun had run out on his partner after all. If a man was sick or had an arrow or two in him, you wouldn't leave him because his mind was all upset. Maybe gold was a sickness too. The question was, did a man ever get over it?

Shaun sat in a scowling study, looking down on the shining beaver ponds.

He thought he had been honest enough when he picked the hollow in the sand to bury the gold; the grass had indicated that it was a place that had been bare of sand for a long time. But Shaun could remember how he had seen the face of the dunes changed each time he passed there, ridges whipped away by the wind and built in a different shape, vast hollows showing high on the slopes of the sand where before there had been long swells and humps.

How honest had he been, after all? Had he figured somewhere in the back of his mind that the sand would take the gold and relieve him of a nameless worry associated with it? Then those long days of stalling at Gondora's place . . . Shaun did a little mental squirming. It could be that he had been deliberately waiting so that the wind and sand would give him an excuse to keep him from changing his life.

Sure, he would have taken his share of the gold if it had been accessible when he and Rainbolt went back to the dunes. Then, being a rich man and a white man, Shaun would have felt obliged to act like one. He would have gone east, back to a life where gold was the supreme measure of a man.

Shaun cornered himself. The chances were that he had cheated Rainbolt without consciously intending to do so, and he had mighty near killed Rainbolt in the bargain.

By now no telling what had happened at the dunes.

Rainbolt was no pork eater. Under most conditions, he could take care of himself even against a man like Frank McCracken. But could he protect himself while half his mind was worrying about gold?

Shaun got up. His knees popped. He stamped his legs savagely as if to rebuke them. Last week two squaws in Rico's camp had made double-edged remarks about stiffness when they heard his joints creak. By God, he was not getting old! Anyway not so old that he could justify running out on a partner. That was just about what he had done, too.

The trouble was, he was not used to studying out such problems. He had been thinking himself dizzy. He would let it all simmer down and see how he felt tomorrow or the next day; and then if he was still discontented and growly with the world, maybe he'd ride back and see how Rainbolt was doing.

CHAPTER SEVENTEEN

Pain has its bearable point, and after that the human body takes measures of its own to shut off the agony. It was that way with Rainbolt now, his third day inside the constricting shell. The pulsations of pain no longer came from any given part of his body; they were, instead, waves swarming over him from all directions. Then the blackness would come and he would be all right. He measured the intervals of suffering by the length of time the sky held its clear blue color. When it began to fade to a haze, he knew the blackness was coming again.

When he was conscious he struggled, trying to free his head. If he could get his head loose perhaps he could slew around and break the rawhide which held his feet to the base of the aspen. Then he could roll down to the creek and let the water soak the hide until it was flexible enough to let him bend forward and chew the bonds on his wrists.

He wished he had thought of the plan when his strength was greater. He kept jerking his head, trying to rip out the pegs at the end of the rawhide thongs around his neck.

His efforts seemed weaker each time he surged against the thongs. Blood ran from his neck. The flies came in an obscene swarm. He did not know at once when he tore out the first stake, for he was unconscious a moment after it came loose.

When he realized what he had done, he lifted into a frenzy of effort. He rocked over on the spruce boughs to get as much slack as possible in the thong, and then he rolled the other way, clear off the boughs. The rawhide cut deeper into his neck. He was strangling when the weight of his body slowly tipped the peg and pulled it from the ground.

He lay for a time trying to gain strength. Ants bit him. Flies crawled on his wounds. Slowly he gathered the will to make the next try. He hooked his tortured, swollen fingers in the bonds at his knees. Rocking from side to side, he hauled back with the desperation of hope. The downhill position of his body helped.

He heard one of the thongs at his feet break with a sodden thump. Fighting against creeping blackness, he put the last of his strength into one more surge against the weakened ties. They broke. He slumped into a stupor.

Sometime later he was dimly aware of being alive. He relived his whole struggle before he realized what he must do next. He rolled toward the creek. His body gained speed. The cool splashing of the water came closer. He could taste it, he could feel it on his body, the blessed water of the little stream.

And then he knew that he was jammed against the aspens, his legs fouled in tough bushes, his neck thongs tangled in the stubby limbs of a fallen tree. He could not roll uphill.

His struggles to roll farther downhill wedged him tighter between the trees until he knew he was at last trapped and helpless, with his strength completely spent.

He could feel the cool breath of the stream only a few feet away. He could see the gracious sky.

Sometime later he heard McCracken and Green River coming back, running in swiftly. They had brought their horses this time. They raced down to where Rainbolt lay with his eyes closed. He tried to gain strength to give them a jeering smile, to insult them, to die like a Sioux warrior.

They fumbled with his bonds. They spoke in excited Spanish. Rainbolt opened his eyes wearily and saw a dim face floating above him, a flash of a knife that went somewhere behind his head.

"Paisano," he muttered. In God's name, no! It could not be! "Paisano!" he cried weakly.

"Be quiet! They return!"

It was Paisano. Rainbolt tried to reach out to her but his hands were still bound. Someone was tugging at his ankles, someone who worked with a jarring of breath that was almost a whimper. Rainbolt's legs fell apart suddenly and the agony of muscles long cramped made him groan.

He was tugged and turned and dragged. There was a dry scraping at his back. Paisano said, "Careful with the knife," and then, more sharply, "Take care, Chico!"

The hide was secured with its own strips. After Paisano and Chico cut it, they could not get it off Rainbolt without scraping him cruelly with the flinty edges of it, and so they slipped it down his body and over his feet. It snapped tight again after it was off him. It rolled against a tree and came to rest. It looked like the hard shell of a dead crawling insect.

Rainbolt still could not get a full breath. "Cut it loose!" he muttered.

"It is gone," Paisano said. She cut the blood-dark rawhide from around his neck.

And Chico, breathing quickly with fear, slashed the bindings on Rainbolt's wrist.

"Cut the hide loose," Rainbolt groaned.

Twigs and rocks were digging into the rawness of his back. Each breath was a hot searing in his lungs.

"The hide is gone," Paisano said.

She watched Chico scamper through the trees to climb up on a rock from which he could see the dunes and part of the trail down the mountain. He was there only a moment and then he came running back as fast as he could, his large brown eyes wide and fear-stricken as he looked at Paisano. "They come!" He fell over the hide. It made a dull rattling noise as it rolled away from him. Chico leaped up and ran toward his horse.

"Come back!" Paisano's voice crackled with authority. Chico hesitated with one foot in the stirrup. Paisano pointed to Rainbolt's rifle hung muzzle down from a thong tied to the limb of a tree. His pistol and shot pouch and powder horn were hung there also. "You will carry those, Chico."

She figured well on the boy's fascination with firearms. Even in his terror Chico steadied himself enough to run toward the weapons.

"First you will help me load him," Paisano said. "Quickly. Do not stare at me."

"They come!" Chico whimpered; but he

ran to help Paisano.

Together they put Rainbolt on Paisano's pony. They could not lift him so they dragged him downhill by the arms to the edge of a steep bank above the creek and then they led the horse below and hauled Rainbolt belly-down across the saddle. His ankles and knees bled and his wrists dripped blood into the stream as he lay across the horse.

Paisano dropped an underskirt and spread it over his back. Chico ran back to the camp for the weapons. He wished to take more of what he saw lying around but any moment he expected the two who had tortured Rainbolt to come bursting through the trees. Chico muttered, "*O, madre, O, madre!*" and scurried back to his horse. He tripped over the long rifle once and the straps of the shot pouch and powder horn almost tripped him again as he rose, but he got the gear on the animal and leaped up to follow Paisano.

They went down the creek, bearing away from the trail as much as they could.

The night before while coming down the trail, Paisano had heard the cries of a man, a man calling out in agony. Chico had wished to go back home then, but Paisano had made him stay with the horses while she crept down through the trees. She was afraid to go close to the camp, but she had got near enough to see that which made her heart turn in compassion for Rainbolt and her blood run cold in hatred of the evil ones who had him.

One of them was McCracken, whom she had fought once like a wildcat when he tried to drag her away with him.

It had been a long night for Paisano, for during the darkness the faint cries had come several times while she huddled in the rocks with Chico. And then this morning they had been forced to wait until the evil ones went away; and after that, while creeping in slowly to be sure both men were gone, Paisano had heard Rainbolt groaning and calling to the One Above for help.

Now he lay like dead across the saddle.

She made Chico tie the weapons to the saddle of his pony and go on foot to keep Rainbolt's head from banging into trees. Several times the injured man started to slide to the ground. Chico grabbed him, clinging hard, crying out for help.

During one of the silences broken only by their own panting and Rainbolt's groans as they pushed him back across the horse, they heard the sound of pursuit behind them.

Paisano led on. She prayed mutely to the God the priest spoke of, to the kind God who was always close to the great altars and banks of shining candles in the churches of Santa Fe and other places where Paisano had never been.

Occasionally she caught glimpses of two men walking on the shallow sand at the dunes. They would help her if she could reach them. They would have to help her. She tugged the horse into a trot when she reached the thinning trees near the foot of the pass. Casting glances behind him so that he often stumbled as he leaped along, Chico still stayed beside the horse that carried Rainbolt.

Paisano vowed that Chico would never go back to his uncle. He had become her brother for what he was doing to save the man she loved. Even if they lost she would still give her life for Chico.

She heard a dry limb break as the pursuers came on. The evil ones were closing now. They must have seen that it was but a woman and a scared boy who had stolen Rainbolt from them.

"The pistol, Chico! Fire the pistol!" Paisano meant it to be a signal to the two men on the sands.

Chico cut the pistol loose from where it was bumping at the saddle horn. He held it in both hands. He closed his eyes and fired it in the direction of the pursuers. It almost jumped from his grip and the powder fumes made him cough. He fired again, and then he turned and raced after the horses.

The attention of the men on the sands jumped toward the pistol shots, but they did nothing except stand and look. Paisano shouted. The men looked. She burst from the trees and urged the pony toward them as fast as she dared. One of the men raised a rifle and stood watching her.

Here in the soft sand with deliverance so close she took a chance and ran beside the horse, shouting at it and slapping it with her hands. It broke into a run. When Rainbolt started to slip she could not hold him. They both fell together and the sand coated Rainbolt's chest with a pale brownness.

Chico ran up beside them and halted, trembling and pale, but he still held the big pistol in his thin hands, and he stayed beside Paisano and Rainbolt as the horse ran on.

"Give me your knife!" Paisano said.

She crouched in the sand, holding the knife and watching the trees. She saw movement there but no one came out. The two men on the sand were striding toward her. All at once Paisano realized that the chase was over. Gently she tried to brush sand from Rainbolt's chest.

He opened his eyes. He knew her. "You will be safe now," Paisano said, smiling.

He felt the sand beneath him. He turned and pushed himself part way up with his hands, staring wildly toward the high dunes. He muttered something about gold and tried to crawl, but his arms collapsed and he plunged face down into the warm sand as the two men walked up.

Back in the trees, McCracken said, "Put that rifle down, you fool! What good is he dead?"

"We can take him away from them," Green River said. "I bluffed Hudson and two of his —"

"Let him go. It didn't work. He'd 'a' died inside that hide before he talked. He'll stay around after they fix him up, and he'll still lead us to the gold." McCracken watched Paisano. He smiled to himself.

In his excitement and relief Chico lost his fear of his uncle. He brandished the pistol. "They chased us and I killed them!"

Aragon snatched the pistol and cuffed the boy. "You! Always in trouble." He started to put the pistol under his belt. All at once Paisano's knife was pressing against his stomach. Her eyes were blazing.

"Do not strike Chico again, never again, Roman Aragon. Paisano will kill you." She took Aragon by surprise. She grabbed the pistol from his hand and tossed it back to Chico. As she stepped back Aragon was outraged to see that she had pricked his stomach with his own knife.

Hudson said angrily, "What's going on here? What happened to this man?" He kept staring at Rainbolt and then he said, "I know him. He's the man —"

"He needs help, Señor Hudson," Aragon said quickly. What was a woman, a knife, a worthless nephew, to interfere with important matters? The injured man was Rainbolt, who knew where the gold was. "We must take him to the *rancho,* Señor Hudson. He has been hurt."

"Why, yes," Hudson agreed, "I suppose so." He gave Aragon a worried look. Sometimes it seemed that Aragon, not John Hudson, was running affairs.

Rainbolt's body had undergone many punishments in his life; it was as tough as any physical tissue could be. But his mind kept betraying him. He thought he was still being choked to death with hide, and he fought away anything that touched his chest. There were moments when he saw both Gail Hudson and Paisano beside him. He spoke to them rationally, but afterward he had no memory of this.

There was a dark, terrible worry riding him, something that he must do, something that he could not do while lying trussed, dying by degrees inside a hot cow hide.

During the second afternoon that he lay in John Hudson's bed his mind began to focus once more. He knew what was worrying him, the gold. Paisano was there alone with him. He asked, "Is the wind blowing?"

Paisano shook her head.

Rainbolt looked at his chest. The pain of raising his head put hot wires in his neck but he looked at his chest to be sure at last that he was free. He was smeared with an ointment that had a pungent odor. There were marks on his wrist that would leave scars. His fingers moved reluctantly.

"There is no wind?"

Paisano shook her head.

Gail came into the room. Rainbolt saw the two women clearly side by side for the first time, the dark one with the heaviness of Cheyenne features refined by Spanish blood, and the tall blond woman with the golden skin.

"How do you feel?" Gail asked gravely.

"I'm all right. My thanks to you both. Where's your father, Miss Hudson?"

"Outside."

"And Aragon?"

"He's watching the men in the field." Gail looked at Paisano and something passed between them that Rainbolt did not understand.

Paisano shook her head. "The gold can wait. You are almost dead from it now."

"How do you know about the gold?"

"It seems that everyone knows," Gail said.

Rainbolt said, "Did I babble while I was sick?"

"Not of gold," Gail answered. "You talked about walking in the rain."

"I'd like my clothes."

"You're in no condition —" Gail stopped as Paisano rose and went to a cupboard. Paisano returned with Rainbolt's pants and boots. She put the pistol beside them on a chair moving quietly, not speaking.

Gail said, "I'll get you a shirt." She returned with one of her father's shirts and put that on the bed. Both women left the room.

Rainbolt started to get out of bed. His leg muscles screamed a protest, but he forced himself to sit up. He swung his legs out and his feet hit the floor as if he had no control over them. Sweating and dizzy he stared down at dark-stained bandages around his ankles.

He could not take a deep breath. He fell

back on the bed and after a time he dragged his legs under the covers. He was all right while he was lying down and resting. Gail had started to tell him that with words. Paisano had let him find out for himself.

When he felt a little better he would go kill McCracken and Green River. He should have done that first, before wasting a minute watching the gold. He listened for the sound of wind. Maybe it was not blowing down here, but up at the dunes . . . What was going on there while he lay helpless?

The house was quiet and cool. Somewhere in the distance men were talking. Rainbolt heard Gail and Paisano murmuring Spanish in the next room.

He fell into troubled sleep. He dreamed that the hollow in the dunes was just as he and Shaun had left it. He was walking over to get the gold when a sudden noise roused him.

Hudson had come into the room. "Glad to see you feeling better, Rainbolt." He was polite and composed, but Rainbolt observed how the man's interest in him was tightly set.

"Who are the men who had you in the hide?"

"The last of the bunch that took your horses, Hudson."

Hudson's expression of well being disappeared. "Perhaps we can do something about those men," he said.

"I will."

"They hold some grudge against you?" Hudson asked carefully.

"Yeah," Rainbolt said. "That's it."

Hudson probed some more, never touching directly on the subject that was in his mind. He learned no more from Rainbolt than he already knew. In disgust he went away to report to Aragon. On the way it again occurred to Hudson that his association of late with the overseer was more of a man to his equal than an employer to an employee.

He made a gesture toward self-respect by calling Aragon from the cabin, rather than going inside to see him. They walked down to the corrals.

"I couldn't get anything out of him," Hudson said.

Aragon shrugged. "There are ways to make him talk."

Hudson was horrified by the implication. Aragon saw that much but he saw more also. "Not here. No, not here before the women. Somewhere alone, just me and Rainbolt."

"No!" Hudson said. He licked his lips. "My God, Aragon!" But he was toying with the idea and it was sinking tiny, unclean fingers into his mind.

Aragon smiled to himself. "Perhaps your daughter then? She could learn much from Rainbolt. It is clear that she is pleased with him as a man."

"What do you mean?"

"A woman could learn what we do not know. It is not much to ask of her."

"I won't have my daughter in this, Aragon!"

"No? Then we will have to take Rainbolt away and speak to him in another manner."

Hidden and lost in the dunes was everything Hudson needed, he told himself. The blank spaces in his character, some of which he was aware of, would in some way be filled automatically or glossed over when he had gold for a speedy realization of his great dream.

He told himself that no man could rise to any great position without being hard and ruthless somewhere during the struggle. That lean, close-mouth, ignorant trapper in the house — what could he do with a fortune? Gold and dreams were for men of station and refinement.

Hudson said, "I'll talk to my daughter." He turned away, but before he went two steps he knew that he would not talk to Gail.

He could not. She would reject the proposition with scorn before he ever had it fully stated. She was like her mother; both had the power to make him afraid. Maybe that was why he had never been the man he had wanted to be.

Hudson bypassed the house and went to his chair in the yard. He sat there making himself angry. This time no woman was going to turn him back. He would let Aragon have Rainbolt. The guilt would be Aragon's, not his, for Aragon had made the proposal in the first place.

Hudson would not inquire about the methods. As king of the empire that was within his reach, he would be above such petty worries. He would reward Aragon handsomely, give him enough of the gold to buy himself fine clothes and silver trappings for his horse.

The ambitions of a man like Aragon were small. Give him authority and gaudy raiment and he would think himself a king.

Now, how to get Gail and the Indian woman out of the way? Before long Rainbolt would be hobbling around. These wild men of the mountains were made of iron. Hudson would suggest that the women ride over to the fort. They could take the Mexican boy with them and Hudson would send all his men as an escort.

The rest would be up to Aragon. When the women returned, Rainbolt would be gone, back to search for the gold, back to the mountains — who could say where a wild trapper went?

It all seemed most simple and logical; but when Hudson went toward the house to get one of his last few bottles of brandy to help work out details of the plan, he saw Aragon watching him from the corral, and he wondered if the man's ambition was as small as he had thought. Perhaps it would be well to give Aragon a small share of the gold.

CHAPTER EIGHTEEN

When he could walk again, Rainbolt spent most of the daylight hours limping in the cottonwoods. Sometimes he sat with his back against a tree, watching the northern half of the dunes, the only part of the sand he could see from the ranch. They must know, McCracken and Green River, that the wind held the answer.

They were waiting near the dunes. In a few days Rainbolt would leave by night. After that he would be a shadow stalking them, and one day in bright sunlight, or at dawn — it did not matter — he would find them. Then he could wait out his appointment with the gold, knowing that the greatest threat to it was removed.

Aragon and Hudson were lesser problems. Aragon was as crafty as a weasel and you could not trust him as far as you could flip a pebble from your thumbnail. His oily good nature meant nothing. Aragon knew the gold was in the dunes.

Hudson was rotting away before Rainbolt's eyes consumed by the very thought of the gold.

Early on the morning that Gail and

Paisano were going to the fort, Rainbolt stood watching the Escobars saddling up. Paisano came to him and said, "I have no wish to go to the fort."

"Gail needs you along for company."

"She needs no other woman around her." Paisano glanced toward the house. "It is her father's wish that she go. There is a soldier at the fort who —"

"I know, Lieutenant Merriam."

"Do you wish me to stay?"

"Go make the visit, Paisano."

"Before, her father has not liked this soldier. Is it not strange that now —"

"I need no help, Paisano," Rainbolt said. Then he remembered when he had needed help desperately and she had given it, and he wished to soften his words, but Paisano had turned away and was going toward the house.

He helped Gail into her sidesaddle later when the party was ready to go. She gave him an odd look and attempted no advice, but there was a moment when she glanced from the house to Aragon, who was mending a saddle in the doorway of the cabin, and back again to Rainbolt.

"It's a long ride," he said.

"Yes, I know. We'll be back day after tomorrow. Will you still be here?"

"I figure to be here, yes," Rainbolt said.

He watched the group go out of the yard. Chico was full of bounce, sending his pony out ahead until Diaz yelled angrily at him.

Not long afterward Hudson saddled one of the sorrels. Rainbolt heard him tell Aragon, "I'm going over by the lakes to see if any cows strayed down that far."

"Do you wish me to go, Señor Hudson?"

"No need. I'll be back this afternoon."

All cut and dried, Rainbolt thought. Hudson had rotted away farther than he had thought. What did they think Aragon could extract from Rainbolt that a shrinking cow hide could not squeeze out?

Aragon played it slowly all morning. He did small chores around the corrals. He sang to himself. He was a simple Mexican with no malice or treachery in him.

In the afternoon Rainbolt was sitting in Hudson's chair under the cottonwoods when Aragon came across the yard, humming a love song. He was carrying a coiled rawhide riata. He was careful to stay wide of Rainbolt, coming in from the side when he approached.

"I will show you, Señor Rainbolt, tricks of roping that I learned long ago on the Baca Grant when I was a boy."

Rainbolt yawned and leaned back in the

chair. "Go ahead."

Aragon made a simple cast and caught a limb snag on a tree twenty feet away. He rippled the rope and flipped the noose free. He caught the snag again with an underhand cast, hopping and grinning as he made the throw. He pivoted from the side and sent the loop no larger than a plate to snap over the limb stub.

Rainbolt had to admit that the riata was a living, flowing extension of Aragon's hands and wrists.

"And now to catch the horse that is suspicious of riatas." Aragon grinned. "One that watches from the corner of his eyes, then twists and dodges his head behind the other horses when you try to rope him." He moved closer to the snag, shaking out the riata carelessly. He put his back to the snag and caught it with sudden cast over his shoulder, turning only his head.

Aragon laughed, deeply appreciative of his own skill and humor. Rainbolt laughed with him, meanwhile keeping his head firmly against the tall back of the chair, keeping his feet on the ground, keeping his hands on his legs close to his pistol.

"It is a good day for showing my skill." Aragon leaned against a tree, letting his loop lie in the dead leaves. "Perhaps if we had a small drink from Señor Hudson's bottles . . ." He glanced in the direction Hudson had gone and then he gave Rainbolt a shrug and a conspiratorial grin.

"Sure, I guess he wouldn't mind." Rainbolt made hard work of rising. "I'll get a bottle." He hobbled as he turned his back and started around the chair.

He took two stops before he heard the rustle of Aragon's loop across the leaves. Rainbolt did not try to duck or to leap aside. He turned with his pistol in his hand and shot Aragon in the chest. At the same instant the loop of the riata fell over his shoulders and slid down to his arms, and the feel of it made his skin prickle with a thousand tiny shudders.

Aragon staggered back against the tree. His mind still set, he tried to jerk the loop tight. Rainbolt shot him again. Held by tremendous vitality and the bracing of the tree, Aragon put his hand on his knife. That was as far as he got. He doubled slowly and then fell loosely to the ground.

Rainbolt flipped the loop from around his body. Aragon was dead, one hand lying on the riata that had failed him. Let him lie there until Hudson found him. Let Hudson, who was in this foulness to his ears, bury Aragon when he returned, and let him make such explanations as he could to Gail and Paisano.

There was a strange silence in the grove. Rainbolt got his rifle and went away, holding close to the hills, going toward the dunes. The gold would keep. First, there were Green River and McCracken.

He went slowly, testing his healing body. A wind began to rise. He saw the banners of its dust leaping in the valley. It rose in the stiff, short-limbed piñons. It came shouldering from the southwest with mighty power.

Rainbolt began to walk faster.

Up on the dunes he saw pale streamers lying against the sky. The wind struck in full force and broke into crazy patterns that filled the air with dancing sand. Rainbolt crept down close. He heard the weird singing of the dunes, the fierce, lonely song of the ages. He could not see clearly what was happening out on the mound where the gold was buried.

A slashing, furious rain followed the wind. Rainbolt huddled under a piñon. He saw the sheets of moisture slanting against the dunes in the misty light. Thunder exploded in the Blood of Christ Mountains, and somewhere far away in the purple mountains to the west there came an answer, as if the mountains were talking to each other.

The wind decreased. For fifteen minutes longer the rain held on and then it was gone with a gentle sigh. The sun came out and showed the dunes a darker brown now, impassive mountains of sand beginning to send vapor into the air.

Out where the gold lay the sand was deeper now. There was a ridge that had not been there before. Rainbolt settled down with a curse. If the wind could move that much sand in so short a time, what might happen when the wind blew steadily for hours?

He could not afford to go after McCracken and Green River. Sometime when he was high on the mountains, the wind might start swirling and eating into the sand, digging out the hollow that had once been there. The gold would lie exposed and he might be too far away to reach it before something happened.

No, he could not go away.

John Hudson returned to his ranch reluctantly. He was afraid of what he would hear and yet there was a squirming eagerness in him to hear it. He went straight to the house for a drink, expecting Aragon to come to him with a report. Aragon did not come. Hudson looked in the cabin. He called out.

There was no answer.

It occurred to him that the worst had happened: Aragon had got the information from Rainbolt quickly and had gone alone to the dunes. Hudson got back on his horse and started out of the yard.

He saw Aragon then. He had ridden past him when he arrived, but his eyes had been on the cabin. Hudson was shocked. He looked around him in terror, expecting to hear Rainbolt's cool voice, expecting to see him step from behind a tree any instant.

The silence accused him.

After a time Hudson used his horse to drag Aragon down to the edge of the potato field. He worked furiously to bury him and then he covered the marks of dragging as best he could. There had been a quarrel and he had fired Aragon and the man had gone away. That was it. No, his horse was still here.

A glib explanation of every detail would make Gail more doubtful than ever. Let Aragon's horse remain where it was. *I rode over toward the lakes to look for cows. When I came back, both Rainbolt and Aragon were gone. That's all I can tell you.*

Hudson went on the trot to the house to get a drink. His horse wandered down to the corrals, reins dragging. After an hour Hudson staggered across the yard to unsaddle the animal. His body was unsteady but his mind was not drunk.

He knew Gail was not going to believe anything he said.

Why had those miserable trappers ever come here with gold in the first place?

Hudson returned to the house and tried to get himself drunk on the last of his brandy. He drank it all.

Lieutenant Merriam helped Gail to the saddle after Colonel Columbine had told her good-by. Soldiers were watching, and the knowledge of that embarrassed Merriam. At the last moment he found courage to say, "A courier came in early this morning. I won't be getting a transfer."

"Oh, I'm sorry, George."

"So am I. I had something in mind that concerned that transfer."

"Oh?" After a moment Gail faltered before Merriam's direct gaze. He was not the uncertain boy she had been taking so lightly all along. He had developed with the demands of a hard life and a savage country. One of these days he would overcome his shyness and she would have to meet his questions squarely.

The sorrel under her sidled and tossed its

head. She took the cue from it and said good-by to Merriam and rode out to join the others waiting to go through the gates. Chico rocketed away in the lead, throwing dust on two disgusted privates at the gates.

One of them spat and cursed.

"Quite a piece," the other said, watching Gail riding away.

"I'd settle for the Indian gal."

"Six months more and Sergeant Mulligan will look good to you, Johnson."

The privates closed the gates.

Lieutenant Merriam walked back slowly toward his hot, cramped quarters.

CHAPTER NINETEEN

On the third day of high wind Paisano came to Rainbolt with food. She was so close before he heard her that he almost shot her even after the crackling instant of recognition. He was gaunt and savage and not fully recovered from his ordeal in the hide.

Paisano put the sack of food down. "They still watch?"

"They're still around."

The woman glanced at the bones of a rabbit the ants were polishing bright. Rainbolt had killed it with a rock at dusk one day and had cooked it over a tiny fire deep in a juniper thicket at night.

"What did Hudson say about Aragon?" Rainbolt asked.

"He said that both you and Aragon went away — where he did not know. That is all he said." Paisano paused. "You killed him?"

"Yes."

"But you did not kill Hudson."

"He's Gail's father."

"Yes," Paisano said, and there were many ways to take her meaning.

"He's learned a lesson, I think."

Paisano seemed to forget the subject. "I

will stay here with you."

"No. It's dangerous."

"I will stay. One of us will always be awake, so that you are not captured again."

"Go back to the ranch! I don't need anyone with me!"

"This gold — what is wonderful about it?" Paisano was honestly puzzled.

"Go away, Paisano. They may have seen you come here."

"No one saw me." Paisano studied Rainbolt. "Would you let Gail stay if she came?"

Her directness startled Rainbolt. "No! Go back to the ranch, Paisano!"

"I go."

After she had gone Rainbolt changed his lookout. For a time he could not get his mind off Paisano and her childlike questions. Then he saw that the wind was coming from the valley again and he forgot everything but the dunes.

This time there was no rain. The branches of the cottonwoods waved and tossed before the steady power of the wind. The dunes cried out their strange song as the sand swirled and lifted and fell.

Rainbolt saw a tremendous hollow being scooped out high on the dunes where there had been long ridges and plunging slopes a short time before. Dusk came and he was not sure of what had happened out there above the gold. After dark he ventured out to investigate, circling away to the west of the cottonwoods.

The long wind was still rolling but not with great force. His footsteps whispered in the sand. He heard the moaning of the wind high on the ridges. Stumbling through the night, he made a wandering, scrawling trail upon the dunes. When he returned to the grove of cottonwoods, he was sure of one fact: the wind had increased, rather than lowered, the sand above the gold.

He slept in a clump of junipers. McCracken and Green River might get in close enough to kill him but not close enough to surprise him and take him alive again.

At daylight he saw that his tracks out on the sand had been blown over.

Gail came looking for him that morning. She rode back and forth through the piñons, along the slopes of the hills, and down through the cottonwoods. She never would have found him, but she was making his presence obvious, and she was too stubborn to go away.

Rainbolt stepped out in front of her horse when she came around a giant *piñon*. He grabbed the bridle of the sorrel roughly.

"Damn it! You know the kind of men that are hiding out around here. One of them instead of me might have —"

"But it was you. I guessed about where you were from what Paisano said." Gail dismounted. She studied Rainbolt critically. "What does *paisano* mean, by the way?"

"Roadrunner. What are you doing here, Gail?"

She looked at the dunes. "My father lost his head completely over the gold. Aragon lost more than that. What about the men on the pass, Jim?"

"What about them?"

"You and Shaun killed some of them. Chico says —"

"That may be only a start. I've got a fortune out there and I aim to have it."

"And then?"

"What does a man generally do with money?" Rainbolt asked.

"It depends on the man." Gail watched him steadily. "There are other things besides gold which you may never see again," she said softly.

It was an open moment for Rainbolt to tell her what she wanted to know, a time to speak directly. He stared at her sharply for a time and turned away. "I'll consider other things when I have the gold."

"Thinking of it has finished ruining my father. What is it doing to you?"

"I'm all right. I know what I'm doing."

"That's nice." The woman said tonelessly. She gave Rainbolt a package of food. She got on the sorrel unaided and rode away.

The winds of the afternoon made Rainbolt uneasy. He knew then the fear of deer and elk during high winds when their senses of smelling and hearing were overridden by natural forces. Twice he changed his point of lookout.

There was fury on the dunes. He watched ridges melt away and hollows appear. Toward evening the wind lessened. In all the immensity of sand there was such a likeness of general pattern that it was hard to believe that anything had changed.

In a moment of humbleness that was frightening he wondered why he, a man whose lifetime would pass like the brief drift of fog in a forest, should think the forces of nature would coincide with his wishes.

But he stayed where he was. Others were staying too, and perhaps he was fighting mortal enemies more than he was the uncaring, unyielding mountains of brown sand.

Once more Paisano came. Once more Rainbolt let down the hammer of his rifle and felt tenseness give way to relief and anger when she called his name softly from the darkness.

"I told you to stay at the ranch."

"I am with weariness. My moccasins are worn." Paisano sat down with a sigh. "I have stolen three of their animals, the horse that was yours and two mules that belonged to the trader Gonzalo Sedeno."

"McCracken might have caught you!"

"He did not catch me."

Rainbolt knelt beside Paisano. "Why did you do this?"

"You cannot go away without horses."

"I'm not going away until I have my gold."

"*My gold*," Paisano mused. "Once it was yours and Shaun's. You say *my gold* but it belongs to the sand now. Shaun knew this at once but you are a fool." She rose. "I go back to the horses."

"Where are they?"

"Against the hills where they will find grass for a time. I will watch them."

"No! McCracken will trail them and —"

"He will not waste time. He will let someone else watch over the horses. It will be easier for him. He will watch you instead."

That was so. Until they were needed, the animals Paisano had stolen were a burden. Why should McCracken and Green River worry about them until they appeared on the sand?

"You didn't get those horses to carry gold, did you, Paisano?"

"If you wish to think so, then I did." Paisano moved quietly away. Her voice came back sad and mocking, "What gold?"

Rainbolt stared at the darkness. The rounding tops of the dunes loomed enormous against the night. They were five miles wide and at least six miles long and hundreds of feet deep. They had cast a curse upon him. If everyone would go away from here, if he knew beyond doubt that McCracken and Green River had given up, then maybe he too could turn and ride away. The wind of the great blue sky was not going to work for him.

Deep in the dark bosom of the sand the buckskin bags would rot and the gold would smear its brightness through the drab grains that smothered it, and it might be that time and circumstance would never unite to reveal the maddening metal. It was a miracle that Rainbolt had seen that piece of armor after centuries of darkness in the dunes.

Rainbolt sat down. If he went away, there would always lie in his mind the thought that he had gone too soon, the jeering thought that he should have waited one more day, or one more week. Who had the knowledge to say when the hollow would appear again? Who had the courage to leave and believe that it never would appear?

In darkness Rainbolt drank from a spring like an animal that must seek cover before the coming of light. He slept in a thicket of crowded junipers, protected against the sudden clutch of enemies by the dry twigs and branches.

At daylight he was staring out upon the sands, waiting, wondering if he had voluntarily placed himself in the tightening grip of something worse than the cow hide.

Another week? Could he break away then? If he stayed the week, would he pass the point where he could no longer argue with himself? Would he become like the Ute father who had built a lodge beside the River of Lost Souls and waited for his drowned son to reappear, and waited until he starved to death?

The wind started early in the morning. It sharpened the dark-spined ridges. It came in howling rushes, breaking and shifting as it screamed across the contours of the dunes. In some places Rainbolt could see quiet spots where it seemed that the surface of the sand was untouched by the wind, while fifty feet away there might be a disturbance that looked like a thousand giant badgers digging; and then at times the sand skimmed across the dunes like brown smoke.

It occurred to Rainbolt that aside from the outflow of the skirts he had never seen any evidence of the sand encroaching into the valley. The dunes were held within proscribed limits by the same force that had built them. They could be as calm as the waters of a lake on a quiet day, or, as now, wind-torn and tossed and noisy; but, like the lake, they were always confined to one small piece of earth.

There could never be any real change here; there was only futility.

And still Rainbolt sat under a tree and waited, no longer with hope, but with animal stubbornness.

It was afternoon before he knew with certainty that a change was taking place out where the long, deep slope covered the gold. The fact grew slowly, for he could not see clearly at all times through the whirling sand. In moments of clarity he saw a ridge appearing where there had been an unbroken smoothness before.

The wind held on. Sometimes it was a steady roaring. Then there were lulls during which Rainbolt heard the strange singing of the dunes and there seemed to be a new, encouraging tone to the sound. He wanted to run out upon the sand and see what was happening at close range; but he forced himself to stay quietly where he was, to wait.

Through the fury of the blowing sand he caught glimpses of a hollow. It was deepening slowly. The newly built ridge lay between it and Rainbolt so he could not tell how fast the wind was twisting the sand away. In the best of weather the shadings of depressions and ridges so nearly blended that they often appeared as one.

He was sitting far out of line with his sighting marks. The angle made it difficult for him to know how close to the gold the wind was digging. Now that it had started after the grinding days of waiting and hoping, Rainbolt did not want to move, to waste watching time by changing his position.

He estimated that the hollow was growing just a little east of the gold; but if the wind did not relent, it would finally tear its way down to bare rock and then it would work with a rotary action to gouge away the sides of the hollow. The ground had been uncovered once. Why not again?

Rainbolt sweated it out.

At dusk the wind was still blowing. Shadows grew upon the sand and he knew there was a great depression close to the gold.

Darkness and changing temperature did not diminish the strength of the wind.

Rainbolt went out on the sand.

He knew for sure that much of the depth on the skirts had been swept away because at times his feet sank down to rocks. He labored uphill in the dark and knew he was striking the ridge. He plunged down the other side into a hollow. He was tense and breathing hard. His sense of direction told him that the cache was off to the left.

He went that way and came against a steep slope of sand. Following the slope he established the fact that there was a great hollow but it was not down to rock yet. In the darkness, with sand scouring against his face, with the wind bellowing above him and tugging his clothes, Rainbolt all at once felt utterly lost.

With nothing but sand underfoot, bumping against the sides of the bowl as he tried to explore, with his sighting marks lost, he had an eerie feeling that he could be miles away from the gold. He lost for the first time in his life all sense of direction and depth perception. When he fell against a slope that he thought was the relatively low southern side of the hollow, he tried to climb out and discovered that he was wallowing against a steep barrier that kept sliding down on him.

He felt his way through the wind and darkness until he fell over the low ridge he had been seeking. He came out on the west side of the hollow instead of the south side from which he had entered.

The moan of the sand mocked him as he went back to the grove where the wind was lashing the cottonwoods. He knew he should find Paisano and have her bring the horses close. By morning the wind might have undone its work and the gold would be lying bleakly exposed and he would have no way to carry it all away quickly.

He did not go to find Paisano. He could not leave the dunes unguarded now that the big change had started.

All night the cottonwoods tossed and the dunes hummed their song and Rainbolt stared into the darkness. At dawn the wind was still blowing.

Rainbolt searched the pale light to see what he wanted to see. His eyes were raw from the scratching of the sand the night before and from sleeplessness. Out on the dunes the brownness was still spinning and falling. The air was brittle and gritty.

Slowly the light expanded. There was a tremendous hollow in the dunes.

Other eyes would have seen it too. Rainbolt could wait no longer. Once more he went across the sand and plowed his way into the hollow.

He felt a shortness of breath. He heard the pounding of his heart. The depression was down to bare rock. It was twice as large as it had been when he and Shaun cached the gold. Rainbolt stared all around it like a questing animal. No sacks stood exposed.

In the center of the hollow, as before, there was a strange quietness, but the wind was spinning furiously around the slopes.

McCracken and Green River had beaten him to the gold! It must be that. He ran, working along the edges of the steep sides of the bowl, kicking the sand with his feet. Broken on the bare earth he saw the breastplate he had trampled into the sand.

He retrieved his grip on reason and logic. The fragments of armor were lying clear of the sand. He recalled the relation of the breastplate to the position of the cache. The hollow was still east of the gold.

Rainbolt plunged up the low ridge to check the sighting marks. He was right. One steep side of the bowl still reached out eight or nine feet over the sacks. The gold was still here.

All he had to do was wait. The wind was eating steadily into the steep banks. Before long it would hurl away the sand. He crouched down in the quiet center of the bowl with the rifle between his knees.

This was the hardest waiting of all, with the end so near. After a few minutes Rainbolt rose and piled fragments of the armor at the toe of the slope. Even as he put the marker in place he saw the wind sweeping sand away, lifting it and carrying it to some other part of the dunes. Before his eyes the wind was melting the sand away so fast that it appeared as if the little scraps of armor were being thrust slowly by an invisible hand farther into the bottom of the bowl.

He crept up the ridge and looked out across the skirts of the dunes. There was no sign of enemies.

He would collect the sacks first in the middle of the hollow, as far away as possible from the steep, treacherous slopes that might cover the gold again. Then he would carry as many sacks as he could at one time out on the shallow sand. Once there, the gold was safe forever from the clutching hands of the dunes.

If he had a pack mule and a horse here now, everything would be greatly simplified. Without them at the moment, he would still get the gold to safety in spite of McCracken and Green River. Again he peered over the low ridge. It was possible that they were waiting for him to do all the work and then they would try to take everything from him when he started across the pass.

Well, he was not going back across Mosca Pass. He was going north on the west side of the mountains and he would not cross the range until he reached the very end of it.

He watched the sand. He listened to the dunes. The gold came closer to him. Shaun was right. Shaun and gold did not fit together. Shaun would die of memories within a year if he went back across the Missouri to stay. It was not going to be easy for Rainbolt either, but he would have money. You could buy just about anything you wanted with money.

In time he would forget the long blue forests on the mountains, the streams in sunlight, the free-blowing, clean winds, the smell and the feel of a campfire, the distance that was forever a glorious challenge — all the wild freedom that he had loved so well before he and Shaun found nuggets in a stream.

The moment came when Rainbolt could wait no longer. He went to help the wind. He scraped with one foot at first and then he put his rifle down and worked on hands and knees, burrowing like a badger toward the sacks. They must be no more than two feet away under the soft, slippery sand.

He knew he should keep going to the ridge to look for McCracken and Green River, but the nearness of the gold created a frenzy in him and would not let him leave. He dug furiously, half blinded by the grit. Under his knees the sand was being whisked away like fine gravel underfoot in a swift-flowing stream.

Every moment he expected his hand to touch the soft leather of a buckskin sack.

CHAPTER TWENTY

By night Shaun Weymouth came riding out of the valley like a Crow bent on mischief. He passed behind the Hudson ranch and went on until he saw the gloomy bulk of the dunes. He spent the rest of the night drifting along the hills on foot, feeling out the watering places to find Rainbolt's camp, or the camp of his enemies.

By dawn he had located three animals near a spring seep, and knew that someone was sleeping close to them. He went in like a creeping Apache and found Paisano.

She told him everything that had happened. Shaun grunted with displeasure. It looked like he had gone soft and made a fool of himself: Rainbolt was still diseased by the gold. The wind made a steady thrumming in the trees as he talked to Paisano.

"What does he say of the gold, Paisano?"

"That he will find it."

Shaun scowled. "Why have you stayed with him?"

Paisano looked away.

No matter, he knew the answer. "What does he say of you?"

"Nothing," the woman answered in a low voice.

"He's a damned fool!" Shaun said angrily.

Paisano gave him a straight, proud look. "I will wait and see what he is."

Shaun growled something under his breath. He went higher on the hills to get a view of the dunes. By Tophet, the wind had gone mad out there! He could see the edges of a hollow. It might be, it just might be . . .

He saw Rainbolt appear as if he had suddenly been pushed up out of the sand. Rainbolt looked toward the valley, he looked toward the cottonwood that was a bearing mark, and then he dropped out of sight again.

Shaun gave fierce attention to the aspens toward the pass. McCracken and Green River would most likely come from that direction. Shaun gauged the distance and decided he had time to get in position. He ran down the hill to Paisano.

"Bring the mules over to that cottonwood — you know the one?"

She nodded and started toward the animals.

Shaun trotted away through the piñons and cottonwoods. He dropped into a broad gulch, and from there he went slowly and carefully toward the sand.

And then he saw that he was too late.

Two men were stalking the hollow, coming in from the other side of it. He saw them flounder over a ridge and drop out of sight. Through the blowing sand he saw them briefly again, and once more they disappeared. He knew they were very close to the hollow.

Shaun started to level his rifle across a limb. The tree was shuddering in the wind, and so he moved aside and raised his gun again. Nothing but the furious sand was in his sights. A shout might warn Rainbolt, but it would also warn McCracken and Green River. Tensely, but with a steady coldness, Shaun waited.

The first figure came into sight off to the right of the hollow, a man crawling up from behind some tiny wave in the sand that was not even apparent from where Shaun stood. The man was only a dark blot against the brownness for an instant, and then he was obscured by blowing sand.

The second figure rose out of the storm a hundred feet to the left of the first man, on the very edge of the hollow. Before Shaun could get a fair sight on him through the brown mist, the man crouched, and then suddenly he fell, or leaped, into the hollow and was gone from sight.

Now he was Rainbolt's problem. Shaun strained and squinted to get his sights on the other man, but the fellow was lying down, so vaguely seen in the ripping of the wind that Shaun knew he could not risk the shot until the man stood up.

Sand streaming down the high bank directly above him warned Rainbolt. He saw a man in buckskins that were jerking in the wind. Green River. His eyes were puckered tight against the slash of the dunes as he peered into the hollow. In the instant of recognition Rainbolt caught the uncertainty in the man. The sand was streaming away from Rainbolt, flying upward into Green River's face.

Rainbolt fell back and grabbed at his rifle. He was farther from it than he had thought. He saw Green River crouch and step forward to get a better view below him. The sand ran under his feet. To keep from falling headlong Green River had to come plunging down the bank. He was almost on top of Rainbolt before Rainbolt grasped his rifle and started to swing it around.

Green River struck him in a driving sprawl. Rainbolt fired, but he knew that the impact had thrown his rifle barrel far to the side. The collision knocked both men into the sand. Rainbolt heard Green River's rifle go clanging out into the hollow.

They grappled on their knees as the sand betrayed their efforts to rise. They rose together, gripping each other's arms. Rainbolt shifted his grasp and tried to whirl and break Green River's arm across his shoulder. He was too slow in the crippling sand. Green River stiffened and held before he was off balance. His knee crashed into Rainbolt's ribs.

They went down again, clawing in the sand, clawing at each other. Rainbolt Indian-wrestled Green River on his back. He blocked Green River's right hand away from his knife and tried to choke him with the other hand. He thought he was succeeding until he felt Green River tugging at the pistol under Rainbolt's belt, trying to twist it into Rainbolt's belly for a shot. Rainbolt had to let go and fight for the weapon.

In the struggle of wrists and hands, the pistol dropped into the sand. Green River came surging up, grinding his teeth like a badger as he tried to bite Rainbolt's nose. Rainbolt knocked him back with his forearm. Green River twisted and bucked in an effort to throw Rainbolt off him.

And now Rainbolt used Shaun's trick of pitting two legs against one, of shifting weight to lure his adversary into turning the wrong way. Green River made his mistake then. He tried to twist out to the side with the least resistance. Rainbolt rolled with him and got both hands on Green River's throat. He levered up and smashed his knees into Green River's belly.

Straightening his arms, bearing down, Rainbolt forced Green River's head deeper into the sand. Green River's struggles merely put him farther into the smothering softness. His hands clawed at Rainbolt's wrists and forearms. Then gradually their frantic movements lessened, and Green River's hands fell away and he was still, with his head completely buried in the sliding brownness.

Rainbolt staggered away from the rocketing wind at the edge of the hollow, out into the quiet middle of the bowl. McCracken would be close. McCracken would —

McCracken was there, rising at the top of the slope to the east. Rainbolt took two more stumbling steps toward Green River's rifle, and then he saw that the lock had been broken when the weapon fell against the rocks.

He put his hand on his knife case, and the knife was a worthless weapon too, at seventy-five feet.

With sand-tortured vision Rainbolt saw

McCracken's rifle steady against his shoulder.

The report was faint in the roaring wind. The muzzle of McCracken's rifle dipped, and then suddenly there was nothing to the man. He toppled face down on the inslope of the hollow and rolled loosely until he lay still on the bare rock bottom of the bowl.

Rainbolt ran and dragged McCracken's gun from the bank. He spilled sand from the barrel and looked at the cap. He ran back to the south side of the hollow and crouched, peering toward the cottonwoods.

Shaun was standing over there. He was just finishing reloading his rifle. Up the gulch, by the lightning-withered cottonwood, Paisano was waiting with two mules and a horse.

Rainbolt stood up, shouting. Shaun raised his hand. They walked toward each other across the rippled brownness.

When they met, Rainbolt did not know what to say. Thanks would have earned him a scornful glare from Shaun. For the first time Rainbolt forgot, at least for a few moments, about the gold.

Shaun rested the butt of his rifle in the sand. "How you been, boy?"

"Good. You just come out of the San Juan?"

"Last night." Shaun glanced toward Paisano. "Wind uncover it yet?"

"Just about." Rainbolt paused. "Made a fool of myself thinking you'd cheat me, didn't I?"

"Yep," Shaun answered.

Shaun glanced at Paisano again and then at Rainbolt and there was a demanding question in his eyes.

"Whatever she wants," Rainbolt said.

"You ain't meaning what you can buy with — ?" Shaun tipped his head toward the hollow.

"No. Whatever else she wants from me."

"None of my business, at that," Shaun said, satisfied. "Let's get the gold."

Rainbolt shouted at Paisano to bring a mule over. He went back to the hollow with Shaun. Shaun looked down unemotionally at McCracken's body. "There's Indians that had more right to put him under than I had."

Over where Green River lay, the wind was racing. Sand had drifted across the body. Rainbolt observed how badly worn the dead man's moccasins were. Shaun picked up a piece of the ancient armor and stared at it oddly before he tossed it away. "Right about there?" he asked, pointing at the slope just beyond Green River.

Rainbolt took a sighting from the ridge. He waded along the curve of it to the west and lined up his objects in the valley. The intersection was very close to where Green River lay. But something was wrong.

The sand was no longer being scoured away above the gold. It seemed, instead, that it was growing deeper. Rainbolt detected nothing different in the course of the wind. He stared at Shaun, who was standing now in the middle of the bowl. Sand was coming down around him in a filmy haze.

Her small feet settling deep as she walked, Paisano came down the low ridge into the hollow, leading a pack mule. She stopped beside Shaun and they both watched Rainbolt.

"It's right here," Rainbolt said. "It's got to be." He began scraping with his foot above the gold. The sand slid in as fast as he pushed it aside. There was still about three feet of the heavy slope extending over it.

Something in the attitude of the two people watching him, an unspoken reluctance mingled with a willingness to help him, made Rainbolt stare at them uneasily.

He turned again to watch the sand. It was creeping out toward the armor fragments, not receding from them. He tossed a handful into the air. It whipped upward quickly and then it fell in a fine, almost invisible spray on the bare ground of the hollow.

The whole bottom of the bowl was sifting over with sand again.

Shaun walked up the low ridge and looked out toward the gulch. Rainbolt noticed how the sand was skimming low against his legs. The ridge was being swept away, and the hollow was being filled again. For a few moments Rainbolt felt rage that this could happen, after the wind had come so close to delivering the gold. To have victory torn from his hands after what he had suffered was almost too much for a man to bear.

He heard the moaning song of the sands. It was neither triumphant nor sad; it was the indifferent voice of the dunes. No sane man could rage against time that did not care and sand that did not hear.

After a time when there was a soft brownness over all the bottom of the hollow, when the sand had hidden Green River's moccasins, Rainbolt pointed toward the gulch and walked away.

Close to the forked cottonwood, he stood with Paisano and Shaun, looking back at the dunes. The dunes had beaten him but there was no dishonor in the defeat; there was only madness in staying on to fight something as powerful and uncaring as a great mountain of sand.

Rainbolt looked at Shaun. "How far toward the San Juan can we be by night?"

"A ways." Shaun's eyes barely moved toward Paisano.

Rainbolt said, "Will you go with me, Paisano? There?" He pointed toward the misty blue mountains.

"Why?" she asked.

"Because you are my woman."

"You are sure of this?"

"Don't you know?"

"I know," Paisano said. "But do you know?"

"Yes. Will you go with me as my wife?"

Paisano gave Rainbolt a last long scrutiny to settle her doubts. She found none, and so she turned toward the horses.

They stopped at the Hudson ranch. Hudson was in his chair in the yard. Fear leaped across his face when he saw Rainbolt, but Rainbolt merely glanced at him and went on toward the house to speak to his daughter.

A young cavalry lieutenant came out with her. George Merriam had ridden most of the night to spend part of the day with Gail, and he would ride most of the night again to get back in time for duty.

"Oh, yes, Rainbolt," he said, when Gail introduced the two men. "You're the fellow who had such a time with the two renegades."

Rainbolt thanked Gail for her kindness to him, and then he said, "About Chico — there's a man named Dimasio Gondora on the Huerfano —"

"Paisano and I have talked about Chico," Gail said. "He wishes to stay here. I'll see that he is well cared for." She looked to where Paisano and Shaun were waiting.

"Yes," Rainbolt said, "she's going with me."

Lieutenant Merriam filled in a bad moment. "I understand you buried gold in the dunes."

"It's there forever," Rainbolt said.

"I see." Merriam studied the packs on the animals. He did not quite believe Rainbolt.

Afterward, he stood with Gail and watched the riders slipping into the distance of the valley.

"What's out there, George?" Gail's voice was cool; but Merriam knew there was a break in her spirit, a hurt and a loss that would leave remembrance he could never share.

"A life we don't quite understand," he said softly.

They were going back to the house when

Hudson rode past them with a short-handled shovel tied behind the saddle. He went out of the yard briskly and turned toward the dunes. He was a lost man, Gail knew, and there was no longer anything she could do to help him. Perhaps there never had been.

She looked at Merriam — a sturdy, determined man, but a man with deep-running gentleness in him.

Far across the valley Rainbolt rode with Paisano at his side. She was not a squaw to drag along in the dust behind him. No matter how she had followed him to dunes and stood in patience when the madness of gold was on him, she would not have gone anywhere with him at the last, he knew, until she was sure that she was wanted.

Blue mountains lay ahead. The dunes grew smaller. For some miles now, Rainbolt had not twisted around to look back at them.

Shaun said, "What are you watching up there in the sky?"

"When I was in that hide, the sky was all I had to look at."

Shaun nodded.

Rainbolt kept taking deep, full breaths. After a time he saw Paisano watching him with a faint smile. He grinned and reached out to touch her hand.

We hope you have enjoyed this Large Print book. Other Thorndike Press or Chivers Press Large Print books are available at your library or directly from the publishers.

For more information about current and upcoming titles, please call or write, without obligation, to:

Thorndike Press
P.O. Box 159
Thorndike, Maine 04986 USA
Tel. (800) 257-5157

OR

Chivers Press Limited
Windsor Bridge Road
Bath BA2 3AX
England
Tel. (0225) 335336

All our Large Print titles are designed for easy reading, and all our books are made to last.